CALGARY PUBLIC LIBRARY

DEC   2017

THE
GOSPEL
OF
MARY

THE
GOSPEL
OF
MARY

A Celtic Mystery

PHILIP FREEMAN

PEGASUS BOOKS
NEW YORK LONDON

THE
WESTERN
SEA

Achill
Island

CONNACHT

ULSTER

Armagh

Boyne R.

Tara

Lambay
Island

Liffey R.

Kildare

LEINSTER

THE
EASTERN
SEA

Aran
Islands

Sleaty

Glendalough

Cashel

Barrow
R.

Emly

MUNSTER

Skellig
Michael

IRELAND

THE GOSPEL OF MARY

Pegasus Books Ltd.
148 W 37th Street, 13th Floor
New York, NY 10018

Copyright © 2017 Philip Freeman

First Pegasus Books edition September 2017

Interior design by Maria Fernandez

Ireland map courtesy of the author.

All rights reserved. No part of this book may be reproduced in whole or in part without written permission from the publisher, except by reviewers who may quote brief excerpts in connection with a review in a newspaper, magazine, or electronic publication; nor may any part of this book be reproduced, stored in a retrieval system, or transmitted in any form or by any means electronic, mechanical, photocopying, recording, or other, without written permission from the publisher.

Library of Congress Cataloging-in-Publication Data is available.

ISBN: 978-1-68177-508-1

10 9 8 7 6 5 4 3 2 1

Printed in the United States of America
Distributed by W. W. Norton & Company

THE
GOSPEL
OF
MARY

Chapter One

The secret to writing is blood.

When calves at our monastery are born in the spring, only the healthy females and a few of the most promising males are kept alive to grow into breeding stock. The rest are slaughtered in the first few months to provide meat for our tables and soft leather for our shoes and clothing. But a monastery is a place of learning and the copying of manuscripts, so the best calf skins are turned into vellum on which we write sacred and secular texts for worship and study.

The actual process of killing calves is a horrible thing to watch and even worse to participate in. The poor creatures are tied with ropes by their hind legs and hung upside down from a low and sturdy branch. The calves are terrified and bellowing for their mothers the whole time, so we try to do everything as fast as possible—hoist them up, hold the neck firmly, knife across the throat—then silence as their muscles twitch and the blood drains away into buckets on the ground. If you're hoping to use the skin for manuscripts, you have to let the blood drain very thoroughly, more than you would if you're just making sausage and shoe leather. If you don't, the pages of your book will have dark veins of dried blood across the surface and won't be fit to write on.

I was thinking about this as I sat at the wooden table beneath the windows of our scriptorium. I was copying the text of one of the psalms onto a sheet of vellum as part of a prayer book we would use in services at the church next door. The manuscript page I was writing on had a few thin and jagged veins across the surface at the bottom. The young novice who had prepared the skins was a dedicated girl, but she hadn't let the blood drain as thoroughly as she should have. I considered fetching a new sheet from the cabinet, but vellum is a precious material and laborious to create. After the slaughter of the calf is done, the skin is soaked in water and lime for days, the hair carefully removed by hand, and the skin tied to a frame and worked for weeks until at last it can be trimmed and cut into pages. You might get two sheets of vellum from a calf skin if you're lucky, so you don't toss one aside lightly. I decided to keep writing.

My pen was cut from a goose quill and my little pot of ink was made from oak galls that we gathered from the forests around Kildare, our monastery on the plains of eastern Ireland that Brigid had founded over fifty years earlier. I dipped the quill into the ink and slowly wrote the lines of the psalm:

> *Shout with joy to God, all the earth.*
> *Sing praise to the glory of his name.*
> *Give glory to his praise.*
> *Say unto God, how terrifying are your works.*

Of course, I didn't spend all my time writing in the scriptorium. There was always so much work to do at the monastery. The sisters and brothers of Brigid were a religious order dedicated to service, so much of our time was spent feeding the poor, tending to the sick, and teaching the children who came to our school. Whether they were Christians or followers of the old ways of the druids didn't matter to us. We were up every day before dawn milking the cows and feeding the pigs, then off to morning prayers in the church. Our abbess Sister Anna and the rest of the women always stood on the left side of the church near the chest that held holy Brigid's bones, with the smaller group of brothers and Father Ailbe gathered on the right. After that a quick breakfast of porridge in the dining hall for ourselves and the widows and children who stayed with us. It was then the real work of the day began, from teaching the children and putting new thatch on the buildings to tending sheep and mending fences outside the monastery walls. After a long day of labor we would have dinner, gather again in the church for evening prayers, then collapse onto our beds. If we had the energy, a few of the younger sisters and brothers might make their way to the kitchen before bedtime for a mug of beer and to trade the latest gossip. It was a good life, though a hard one, serving God by serving those in need.

But it was precarious. A monastery of women and men living and working together as equals was not popular with the church authorities in Ireland nor in Rome. Some monasteries had a few sisters to do the cooking and cleaning for the priests and brothers, but these women were servants, not partners. Most monastic communities kept women away completely out of fear that they would lead the men into sin. It was my experience that the opposite was more likely, but even that was rare at Kildare. We took our work and our vows of celibacy seriously. And honestly, we were too busy most of the time to think about sex.

Brigid, who had died a few years earlier, had fought all her life to keep the bishops from shutting us down. If church politics weren't enough, the monastery faced the constant challenges of poor harvests, disease, war, and threats from the noblemen of the province who coveted our land. It was a miracle that Brigid and her successor Sister Anna had managed to keep the monastery running amid the famine and violence of our island. But as Brigid once reminded me, miracles favored those who worked hard to make them happen.

The sun was dipping low in the western sky and evening shadows were reaching across the room when I finished copying the psalm. The windows of the scriptorium were larger and higher than in the other buildings and faced south to catch as much light as possible for writing. I sometimes copied texts at night, but candles were expensive and the light they gave out was never bright enough. So when darkness began to fall, I placed the vellum sheet on the table with stones weighting each corner so that the ink could dry. I then took the old psalm book I was copying from, placed it carefully back into its leather case, and put it on the shelf in the cabinet with the hundred or so texts we owned. If there were ever a fire in the monastery, we would save the books before anything else. Clothing, farm animals, even holy objects used in the church could be replaced, but—aside from the souls inside our walls—books were the most precious commodity at Kildare.

I walked outside and stood in the doorway looking toward the setting sun. It was one of those rare autumn evenings in Ireland without a cloud in the sky and no threat of rain. I could see our tenant farmers leading cattle to their barns in the fields beyond the walls. To the south was a thick forest of oak where we grazed our pigs on acorns, and the winding path that led to my grandmother's house nearby. Inside the walls the sisters and brothers were busy finishing their chores and getting ready for our evening meal. Across the yard I saw my friend Dari leading her class of young children from the school to the well to wash for dinner. The hut for widows was next to the school and our kitchen stood across from Sister Anna's stone hut. Most of the other buildings, apart from the church, were circular structures like you would see anywhere in Ireland made from woven branches and mud caulking roofed with thick thatch to keep out the rain. The sleeping hut for the brothers was on the eastern end of the compound while the sisters slept in a larger building on the western side. The church itself was made from heavy oak planks whitewashed with lime that shone brightly with the last rays of the sun.

"A peaceful scene, isn't it?" said a familiar voice.

Father Ailbe was walking slowly from his hut to the dining hall. I came down the steps and kissed him on the cheek.

"And what did I do to deserve a kiss from a beautiful young woman?" he asked.

"Nothing special, Abba. I'm just glad to see you, as always."

I had called him Abba since I was a little girl and couldn't pronounce his name properly. Father Ailbe was once a tall man, but over eighty years of life had left him slightly stooped. When his arthritis was acting up, as it was lately, he walked with a slow gait since he refused to use a cane.

I had known Father Ailbe my whole life. He had come to Ireland as a missionary from Alexandria in Egypt when he was in his twenties, a few years before Patrick himself arrived on our island from Britain. Father Ailbe was a skilled physician and gifted scholar as well as our bishop. He conducted our services and taught the older students theology and languages, but he deferred to Sister Anna in all other matters related to the running of the monastery. Even he did not dare to tell our abbess how to manage the affairs of Kildare.

"How goes the copying of the psalter?" he asked.

"Well enough, Abba, though the vellum page I'm using could have been prepared more carefully."

"Ah well, my dear, the Lord doesn't demand perfection, just our best effort. Are you coming to dinner?"

"Yes, but I'm going to wash up first. I've got ink all over my fingers."

Father Ailbe was listening to me, but he was also gazing out over the walls past the eastern gate to the path that led from the woods about a quarter mile away.

"Deirdre, is that someone coming toward the monastery?"

I squinted and saw a small figure moving slowly out of the trees along the path. I couldn't tell who it was at such a distance, but it looked like an old woman dressed in a dark gray cloak.

"It is. A woman I think. But all the sisters are here and we're not expecting visitors. I'd better go and make sure she's all right."

"Yes," he replied. "I'll tell Sister Anna we have a guest for dinner."

I walked quickly across the yard and out of the gate toward the approaching stranger. As I got closer, I could see she was indeed an old woman—and a fellow nun, from her clothing and the wooden cross around her neck. But it wasn't until I was a few feet away and had called out a greeting that she raised her head and I recognized Sister Branwen, a British nun I hadn't seen since she was a guest at Kildare when Brigid was still alive.

She looked exhausted and in pain, grasping her chest. I moved quickly and caught her by the arm as she started to fall.

"Deirdre . . . is it really you?"

"Yes, Branwen. Are you hurt? Let me get some of the brothers and sisters to carry you to the infirmary. Father Ailbe can help you."

"No . . . just let me . . . sit here . . . in the grass," she gasped. I eased her down and took off the satchel she was carrying over her shoulder.

I lay my cloak on the ground for her to lie down on. Her breathing was shallow and she was as pale as a ghost. I don't know how she had managed to walk any distance. I shouted to the monastery for help to carry her inside.

"Branwen, don't worry. We'll take good care of you. The others will be here in a minute."

"Too late," she answered as she lay on her back in the field staring up at me. "Doesn't matter anymore . . . now that you're here . . . I came to find you . . . Deirdre . . . in my satchel . . . leather case."

I rummaged through the few belongings she had in the bag and found a round leather tube about a foot long. It was similar to the cases Father Ailbe had in the large chest in his hut to store the papyrus scrolls he had brought from Egypt—dark with age and sealed at the top with wax to keep out moisture.

"Take it. . . . Keep it safe."

"Forget about that now, we've got to take care of you before—"

"No!" she shouted as she grasped my hand with surprising strength. "I don't matter. . . . Keep it safe. . . . They will be coming."

"Who will be coming?" I asked. "Why is it so important?"

It took her a moment to gather the strength to answer me. I could see Brother Kevin and several of the sisters running down the path toward us. I bent down as Branwen held me close and whispered in my ear.

"Deirdre . . . *she* wrote it. . . . They will be coming."

With that, she closed her eyes and let go of my sleeve. She was still breathing, but no longer conscious. Brother Kevin arrived with the others and knelt down beside her.

"Kevin, please carry her to the infirmary right away."

He and the sisters with him rolled up the edges of my cloak and gently carried her between them up the hill to gate of the monastery. She was a small woman and no great burden.

I followed them up the path and inside the monastery walls. The infirmary was on the eastern end of the yard near Father Ailbe's hut. I went inside behind the litter and waited while Kevin and the others eased Branwen onto the examination table on the right side of the hut beneath the medicinal herbs that hung from the ceiling. Sister Anna was already there and had lit several candles to help Father Ailbe better see his patient. I placed the leather case Branwen had given me on a bench in the corner and went to help Father Ailbe.

He placed an old rag pillow beneath Branwen's head and put a woolen blanket over her shivering body. A quick examination told him there were no external injuries. He felt the pulses on her neck, hands, and feet, then gently pulled aside the blanket and her tunic, then put his ear against her chest to listen to her heart and lungs. He tucked the blanket back up to her neck and shook his head. He then asked Kevin to carry her to a bed on the far side of the infirmary.

"Chronic heart failure," Father Ailbe reported to Sister Anna, who had been standing nearby the whole time. "She must have been sick for months. I'm amazed she was able to walk at all in her condition, let alone journey here from Britain. I think she used the last of her strength to come to us. I'm afraid there's nothing that can be done for her except to keep her comfortable. I doubt she'll regain consciousness. She may not make it through the night."

Sister Anna nodded and turned to face me. Our abbess was about sixty years old, a small woman, but I had never met anyone who could command respect like she did. Her dark gray eyes fixed on me and her strong voice reminded me, as always, of when I was a little girl in her classroom.

"What did she say to you, Sister Deirdre?"

"Only that she wanted me to keep this safe." I walked to the bench and brought the leather case, which she examined.

"Did she say anything about what is in this?"

"No, Sister Anna, only that *she* had written it, whoever *she* is."

"May I see that?" Father Ailbe asked Sister Anna, who handed it to him. He looked at the case and ran his fingers over the wax seal at the top.

"This is very old," he said to us. "I haven't seen one like this since my student days in Alexandria. They haven't been used for centuries."

He gently shook the case. There was definitely something inside.

"Branwen was desperate for me to keep this safe," I said to Sister Anna. "She said they would be coming for it."

"Who?" she asked.

"She didn't say."

Sister Anna took the case back from Father Ailbe and looked at it for a few moments before speaking.

"Father, would it harm the papyrus inside to open the case? I would like to know what exactly we're dealing with before I decide what to do."

"I doubt it would do any damage," he answered. "But we must be careful. The scroll is likely to be fragile. I would recommend Deirdre open it. I'm afraid I don't trust my old hands with something this delicate. Besides, I should stay here with Sister Branwen."

Sister Anna looked dubious, but nodded in agreement. "Sister Deirdre, take the case to the scriptorium and find out what is inside. But be very careful. I don't want to damage it, whatever it may be."

"Of course, Sister Anna."

I met Father Ailbe's eyes as I left and he smiled. I was honored that he trusted me so. I took the case and left the infirmary. Just outside the door was Dari.

"Deirdre, what's going on?"

Dari's real name was Sister Darerca, but no one called her that except our abbess. She was the same age as me with long blond hair and bright blue eyes that always seemed joyful. She was my best friend at the monastery. I knew she had a past that should have left her anything but happy, but joy was Dari's gift.

"I'm not sure yet. I'm afraid Father Ailbe says Branwen isn't going to live very long."

"Oh no. I never met her, but how could she make it here from Britain if she was in such bad shape?"

"God knows, Dari. But she gave her life to do it. And it was all for this."

I showed her the case as we walked together to the scriptorium.

"What is it?"

"A storage container for a papyrus scroll. Father Ailbe says it's hundreds of years old. Sister Anna wants me to open it and see what's inside. Branwen said that people would be coming for it."

"Do you mean Branwen stole it?"

"That doesn't seem likely. I knew Branwen when she was here years ago and she was the least likely thief you could ever meet. But somehow she ended up with an old papyrus scroll that somebody wants very badly."

We walked through the gathering darkness to the scriptorium. Once inside, I moved the psalm page I had been copying from the table and took it to a nearby shelf, chose some candles from the basket in the corner of the room, and sent Dari to light one from the lamp we always kept burning on the altar of the church. While she was gone I ran my hands over the case and put my nose close to the skin. It smelled old, but there was something more. Just a hint of the sweet smell of incense.

Dari returned, and I placed the candles around the edges of the table close enough to see whatever I took from the case, but far enough away to keep the flame from the papyrus. The last thing I wanted to do was burn it.

I took a sharp knife I used for trimming the nubs of the writing quills and eased it into the hard wax around the top of the case. The seal was ancient and hardened, but I carefully slipped the blade beneath it and worked my way around the top of the case.

"Be careful, Deirdre."

"I am being careful. I'm nervous enough without you warning me."

"Sorry."

I finished working the blade around the case and loosened the top. Slowly I twisted and pulled the cap from the tube until it made a dull popping sound as it came off. Dari jumped slightly.

The air must have been sealed inside the case for centuries. It was musty and stale, but again with a faint sweet smell. I was sure now it was frankincense.

"What do we do now?" Dari asked.

"I take out the papyrus—very carefully—and see what it says, assuming I can read it. Papyrus was used for writing a lot of different languages."

I placed the case on the table away from the candles and reached two fingers inside. I could feel the tattered edges of the roll. I held it gently between my fingers and slowly pulled it out of the case.

It was certainly old—that I could tell right away. The scroll itself was rolled up tightly and was dark yellow, almost honey-colored. Like all papyrus, it was made of long fibers running up and down as well as across the surface. Papyrus is made from reeds that grow only along the banks of the Nile that are soaked in water for days, then laid out across each other and pounded while wet with a wooden mallet until they form a solid sheet that's then dried. Papyrus scrolls are usually about a foot high and maybe six feet in length. This one was slightly smaller than most, but I couldn't tell how long it was until I unrolled it, a task that terrified me.

When I was a teenager and learning Greek, Father Ailbe had loaned me a papyrus scroll of the poetry of Erinna, a Greek woman who had lived just before Alexander the Great. He had told me to be very careful, since no other copies of her work survived anywhere that he knew of. I was so excited that I took the scroll back to my desk and opened it too quickly. It tore down the middle with an awful ripping sound and some of the lines were lost. Father Ailbe had never raised his voice to me before that day, but I learned then what it was like to see him angry.

I held this scroll in my hands as Dari watched and forced myself not tremble as I slowly unrolled it a few inches. The letters were small and the writing was badly faded.

"Dari, get a few more candles from the basket and put them on the end of the table. There's not enough light to see what this says."

She did as I asked. I held the end of fragile scroll in front of the flickering light.

"What does it say?"

"I don't know yet. It's not in Greek or Roman letters. It looks like Hebrew—no, Aramaic."

"Aramaic?"

"Yes, it was the language of Syria and Palestine centuries ago. Father Ailbe taught it to me when I was younger. It was spoken by the Jews and others when the Romans ruled there."

"Okay, but what does it say?"

"I'm working on it. Give me a moment."

The writing was so faint that it was hard to make out the letters. But after a minute my eyes adjusted to the low light and the writing style of the scribe. At last I could read the first line.

"No . . . it can't be."

"What? What does it say, Deirdre?"

I took a deep breath, then translated it for Dari:

These are the words of Miryam, mother of Yeshua of Nazareth, the one they call the Christ.

Chapter Two

Miryam?" Dari asked. "Do you mean Mary, the mother of Jesus?"

My hands were shaking as I lay the scroll on the table in front of us.

"Yes," I answered. "Miryam was her name in Hebrew. The Greeks and Romans called her Maria. We call her Mary."

"Are you . . . are you saying that this was written by the Virgin Mary almost five centuries ago?"

"That's what the scroll says. But lots of old books claim to be written by someone famous—Homer,

Plato, even the Apostle Paul. Though I've never heard of any book daring to say it was written by Mary herself."

"But what if it's true?" asked Dari.

"Let's not get ahead of ourselves. I want to talk to Father Ailbe and Sister Anna before I translate any more."

I carefully put the scroll back into its leather case and twisted the top on tightly. Returning to the infirmary, we found Father Ailbe and Sister Anna sitting by Branwen's bed. When Dari and I approached, they stood up.

"How is she, Abba?"

"Still unconscious, I'm afraid. Her breathing is shallow and irregular, but she's not in any pain. Praying is all we can do now."

"What did you discover about the papyrus?" asked Sister Anna as she motioned us away from the bed and back to the table on the far side of the hut.

"I opened the case and read the first line. That was as far as I got. I wanted to come back and tell you and Father Ailbe what it says before I read any more."

"Continue," said the abbess.

"It's written in Aramaic, the language of the Jews in the time of Jesus."

"I know what Aramaic is, Sister Deirdre. What does it say?"

"It claims to be a document written by the Virgin Mary."

Father Ailbe let out a slow breath and closed his eyes. Sister Anna didn't change her expression as she stared at me.

"Mary. A document written by Mary herself. No wonder Sister Branwen was so afraid."

"I don't understand, Sister Anna," Dari said. "Why would something written by Mary be dangerous? Wouldn't it be wonderful to have her own words and stories? We could learn so much from her."

"Let's all sit down," said the abbess.

We moved to the hearth in the middle of the hut and sat on the benches in front of the fire. Father Ailbe sat next to me.

"Let us consider this carefully," said Sister Anna. "What we do next could have tremendous consequences, not just for our monastery but for the whole church."

"I still don't understand," said Dari.

"Consider the possibilities," said the abbess. "We have an ancient document that claims to have been composed by the Virgin Mary. Now either it was written by someone using her name or it is genuine. If it is a forgery, it could spread false teaching like the many documents that claim to have been written by the apostles or fathers of the church. There are dozens of gospels, letters, and collections of sayings in circulation claiming to have been composed by important figures in the early church. Some assert that the true knowledge of Christ can only come through secret teachings—which he just happened to have revealed to them alone. Other groups claim that Jesus was only a gifted prophet, not God himself, or not a man at all but a spirit who only seemed to take human form. In any case, they can confuse and lead astray those who are weak in the faith. This document may be one of those. I do not wish to add to the library of false teachings already in circulation."

"But, Sister Anna, what if it's true?" I asked. "What if this scroll really was written by Mary?"

"Sister Deirdre, can you tell the difference between a genuine and false document written centuries ago?"

I turned to Father Ailbe.

"Abba, is there a way to know if this was written by Mary or not?"

I could tell his mind had been somewhere else up to this point. When he was deep in thought, he always pursed his lips together and stared at the floor. But now he looked up at me.

"There is no way to be certain," he answered, "but there are signs to look for. For example, does a story seem to fit the character who claims to be telling it? A peasant woman from Galilee isn't going to sound like a Greek philosopher. Does it contradict in some notable way what we know from the genuine Gospels? Naturally there would be new stories and a different point of view from Mary, but if it portrays Jesus as something radically different from the man we know, then either all our sources are wrong or the author is creating a fictional character."

"That makes sense," I said.

"And then there's the feminine point of view," he continued. "I don't subscribe to the idea that women and men are profoundly different from each other in the ways that they think, but then again they are not the same. A woman tells a story in a different way than a man. Not better or worse, just differently. That could point you at least to whether the author was a man or a woman."

"Yes," I said. "I think you're right. But, Abba, you should be the one who translates this, not me."

He smiled and looked at me as he spoke. "No, Deirdre. I'm afraid my old eyes are no longer able to read faded letters on a papyrus scroll. But aside from that, it isn't my work. I'm not a great believer in fate, but I don't think it's by accident this scroll has come to you. I can't help but believe that Branwen placed it in your hands for a reason." He looked now at Sister Anna and Dari as well. "You see, I have heard of such a document, a Gospel of Mary. I have serious doubts about whether it's genuine, but the stories about it are very old. There were whispers about it even in the Library of Alexandria. The legend passed down through the centuries is that Mary dictated it to a scribe soon before she died. The scroll was supposedly sealed inside a case and passed down among women in the Christian community who kept it hidden and safe through the years. The women who guarded it held it as a sacred trust. It was so revered that no one dared to break the seal and read it, so no one knows what it says. I heard when I was young that the scroll had been spirited away from Palestine when the Romans destroyed the Jewish temple and that it was kept safe by a community of Christian women in the deserts of Egypt for many years. When the Persians threatened the eastern part of the Empire, it was taken to Italy and then to Gaul. If this is indeed that fabled document, then I presume it was sent even farther away to Britain as the Roman Empire began to collapse so that it would be safely beyond the reach of barbarian invaders, not to mention male church leaders. I can only guess that the sisters at Branwen's monastery hid it from the church authorities. And now it seems it has come to Ireland. Again, I will need solid proof before I believe this gospel is genuine, but the one thing I do know for certain about it is that in all the centuries it has been in existence, the church at Rome has been trying to find and destroy it."

"But why?" asked Dari.

"My child," answered Sister Anna, "the leaders of the church fear it because they don't know what it says. Power is always threatened by the unknown. I too have heard of this document. There have been rumors of it for years among the sisters of our faith, even on our island here at the edge of the world. The stories I've heard are much like Father Ailbe's, but were passed down among women. They say that from the beginning, the women of our faith who guarded this gospel swore to give their lives to protect it from enemies outside and within the church—and many did. From the time it was written, the church leaders in Alexandria and Rome sought to track down this document and burn it, along with any women who dared to stand in their way. The priests and officials the church commissioned to find it thought of themselves as good Christians. They took no joy in torturing to death the women they thought could lead them to this gospel. They believed they were doing the work of God—the most dangerous kind of men. They chased it for years through the deserts of Egypt and then at last to a convent in the heart of Rome itself where the holy women who had protected it gave their lives rather than reveal where they had sent it.

"Decades later the church leaders in Rome heard rumors it was in a monastery near Paris, but before they could reach it the Franks invaded and put the place to the torch. Not that the church objected. Better to have the barbarians slaughter the nuns and burn the false gospel than dirty their own hands. But that wasn't the end of it. A single sister escaped Gaul with the scroll and took it to Whithorn in northern Britain where the local sisters guarded it for years. I hadn't heard what happened to it after the Picts destroyed the church there, but it seems it was spirited away to Branwen's monastery, where it must have been ever since. I remember Brigid speaking of it to a few of us while she was still alive. I think she knew where it was, but she wouldn't tell anyone. I believe it was her hope that someday the world would know what it said."

There was suddenly a low gasp from the other side of the hut. We all rose quickly and went to Branwen's bedside. Her breathing was fitful now. Sister Anna gently kissed her on her forehead, an act of tenderness I had seldom seen in our abbess. Branwen took a final breath and was silent. The four of us each placed a hand on Branwen's body and bowed our heads to pray for our friend as she began her journey to the next life.

When we were done, Sister Anna gently pulled the blanket over Branwen's face. Then she spoke to me:

"Sister Deirdre, whether by chance or design this document has come into your hands. I don't know if it is genuine or not, but out of respect for Branwen and all the women since the beginning of our faith who have risked their lives to watch over this scroll, it is now your responsibility. You and I have had our differences over the years and I have grave doubts that your temperament is suited to this task, but Branwen gave it to you alone and I must honor her wishes. You are a bard and can cross the tribal boundaries of this island at will, unlike most of us. You may need to travel far before you can find a safe place to work. You must also be the one for the very simple reason that you are the only person in Ireland, aside from Father Ailbe, who can read Aramaic. Therefore it is yours. You must guard it with your life. But more than that, you must find out what it says."

"But, Sister Anna, what if I discover it wasn't written by Mary at all?"

"Then that too we must know. I believe that Christ founded a church that can weather any storm. If it is a forgery, let that be the end of it. But if these are truly the words of the mother of Jesus, then let the world hear what she has to say."

Father Ailbe nodded.

"But," said the abbess, "you cannot do your work here. Branwen was right that the church authorities will come looking for this scroll. The bishops have been trying to shut down our monastery for years. We cannot give them a reason to do so by protecting you. You must leave tonight, while the other sisters and brothers are at evening prayers. Take what you need and go quickly."

"But where should I go?"

"That I leave to you. Do not tell me or anyone else where you are heading. I want to be able to answer honestly when I say I don't know where you are. We will bury Branwen quietly. As far as I'm concerned, she came here to die among friends." She looked at Father Ailbe. "I never saw any scroll she might have been carrying, did you?"

Father Ailbe shook his head. "No, Sister Anna, I did not."

She then looked at Dari. "Sister Darerca, only the four of us in this room know the truth. You may stay here at the monastery in silence if you wish. But if I know you, I imagine you will want to go with Sister Deirdre."

"Yes, Sister Anna, I certainly would. Deirdre is going to need my help. And besides"—she grinned—"I might be able to keep her out of trouble."

"That I seriously doubt," said the abbess with a stern look for us both.

I held the case with the scroll close to my chest. It seemed heavier now. "I will do as you have said, Sister Anna. When I'm finished, I'll return here and let you both know what I have found."

"I look forward to that day—and I hope I have chosen well in trusting it to you. I shall pray for your safe return. May God help us all." She left the infirmary without a backward glance and went toward the church. Father Ailbe came to my side of the bed and embraced me.

"Deirdre, my child, be careful. The men who will come after you are not to be underestimated. As Sister Anna said, they believe they are doing the will of God by attempting to destroy this scroll. They may come to you wearing sheep's clothing, but they are wolves. Very dangerous wolves."

"Yes, Abba, I'll be careful. I'll be back as soon as I can. And please don't worry. I know how to take care of myself."

Chapter Three

Dari and I left the infirmary and went to our sleeping quarters. We quickly gathered a few clothes and wrapped them in our thick woolen blankets, which we tied around our shoulders. I also took my father's sword from underneath my bed and my harp from the wall. The satchel I stored the harp in was made of waterproof leather, so I put the scroll case into it for extra protection and slung it onto my back. Dari went to the kitchen to find some bread and cheese for the journey, while I went back to the scriptorium for parchment, pen, and ink. We then walked together out of the gates of Kildare into the darkness.

"Where are we going?" asked Dari.

"For tonight, to my grandmother's house. After that I'm not sure."

We took the path south through the woods. It was a moonless night, but I had walked this trail so often I could have done it with my eyes closed. We passed by the spring known as Brigid's Well and I could hear the water flowing over the rocks as it made its way to the clearing among the oaks where my grandmother's hut stood.

Her single cow was in the small barn next to her hut and it lowed softly as we came near. My grandmother didn't have any dogs like most households but lived alone with only her milk cow and a few chickens she kept in the yard. She was used to visitors at all hours, so I knocked on her door and entered. She was sitting by the fire stirring a pot over the flames. She didn't seem surprised to see me.

"Would you two like some soup?"

I took off my blanket, satchel, and cloak, then crossed the room to give her a kiss on the cheek.

"Grandmother, I'm sorry we're showing up like this in the middle of the night, but can we stay here until morning?"

"Of course you can," she said. "Dari, come here and give me a hug."

"Thank you, Aoife," Dari said. "We won't be any trouble."

"Well, that remains to be seen," Grandmother replied.

"Grandmother, we're here tonight because—"

"Deirdre, stop. Have a seat and you both have some soup before you tell me your tale. Did I raise you so poorly that you don't let Dari eat something when she comes into my house?"

I motioned Dari to the bench by the fire and ladled her a bowl of what was boiling in the pot. It was Grandmother's chicken soup, my favorite. The night had turned cool and we hadn't had any dinner at the monastery. It tasted wonderful.

"Grandmother, you didn't seem surprised to see us."

"I'm a seer, young lady. I know all the mysteries of the world. Besides, I was up late making the soup and heard your footsteps on the path. I may not be as young as I once was, but my ears still work fine."

My grandmother was a short woman in her early seventies with silver hair and a twinkle in her eyes. She had been through many hardships in her years, but she seldom showed it.

"So, what brings you two here in the middle of the night with traveling packs on your backs? Did Sister Anna kick you out of the monastery?"

"No, Grandmother. The abbess sent us away, but for good reason."

I told her all that had happened that evening. She listened carefully to everything. Dari ate a second bowl of soup while I talked.

"Mary, the mother of your Jesus? Well now, that is interesting. I'm no follower of your rather odd religion, but even I would like to know what the scroll says."

My grandmother was a druid and the daughter of druids in a line that reached back to the beginning of our people. She was on very good terms with the sisters and brothers of the monastery, but she was a devout follower of the old ways. When my mother had become a Christian as a teenager, my grandmother was livid. But before my mother died just a few years after giving birth to me, she made my grandmother promise her that she would raise me in the Christian faith, which she had.

"So you see, Grandmother, we're just here for tonight as we look for a place to stay and safely translate the scroll."

"You'd be welcome to stay with me as long as you need, Deirdre, but this is the first place they'll look after they find you're not at the monastery."

"I know. I'm sorry if I've put you in danger."

"Ha! Do I look scared? No bully boys from Rome are going to frighten me. If they try, I'll turn them all into toads."

"Can you really do that?" asked Dari, her eyes wide.

"Well, no. But I can make them think I can, which is almost as good."

"Grandmother, forgetting magic spells for a moment, could you look at the scroll and see if you can tell me anything about it?"

I got the scroll out of my harp case and began to twist off the top.

"No, don't take it out. I don't need to touch it. Just hand me the case."

My grandmother couldn't change anyone into anything, but she was a gifted druid seer. The druids were the priests of our people, as they were among the Britons and Gauls across the sea before the Romans destroyed the Order there. Druids performed sacrifices, studied the ways of nature, conducted marriages and funerals, and sought to know the will of the gods. They could be either men or women, but it took years of study and preparation that few of either sex were capable of completing. It was only when the training was done that a druid was confirmed in his or her special calling. For some, it was reading the entrails of animals given as offerings. For others, like me, it was the gift of music as a bard. For my grandmother, it was the ability to see into the past and sometimes the future.

I was raised in the church, but I honored the ways of my grandmother as well and tried my best to walk the difficult path of being both a druid and a Christian. If I had been a sacrificer or seer, it would have been impossible to live in two worlds, but my calling as a bard didn't conflict with my position as a sister of Holy Brigid—or so I told myself. As a bard I sang songs of praise and satire, recited poetry for royalty, and held the history of our people in my memory. I spent years training not far from Kildare with the greatest druids and bardic teachers in Ireland. I was revered by all and was sacrosanct in our land. To kill a bard was to destroy the past and bring a curse on yourself and your family for generations. With my harp in my hand, I could travel wherever I wished on our island and even walk between armies to stop battles. No one would dare to touch me—at least among the followers of the old ways.

My grandmother took the case with the scroll and held it on top of her open palms. She closed her eyes and began to softly chant words I couldn't understand. After a few moments, her eyes flew open.

"Take it, Deirdre," she whispered. "Quickly. I don't want to drop it."

I took the case from her and set it down on the table.

"What is it, Grandmother? What did you see?"

She was shaking and there was sweat across her brow. She sat down by the fire. I poured her a cup of mead from the flask in the corner and handed it to her.

"Are you all right? You acted like it was burning you."

"No, not burning. Something very different." She took a long drink of mead and wiped her mouth on her sleeve. "It was strange. It was like time stopped while

I was holding it. I know it was only a few seconds, but it seemed much longer."

"What did you see?"

"At first, nothing. Then suddenly there was a rush of images and sensations that almost overwhelmed me. There was an old woman sitting outside a hut staring at the setting sun. Then a boy laughing and playing with his friends. Then a young woman screaming in pain as she gave birth. Then a man dying in agony while women near him wept." She put her head in her hands as she spoke. "Deirdre, I've been a seer for a long time, but I've never seen—never felt—anything like that."

"Grandmother, could you tell if it was Mary who wrote it?"

She lifted her head and looked at me. "No, child. I don't know who spoke the words written on that scroll. It was a woman, that I do know. A woman who knew suffering and sorrow beyond what we can imagine. But who it was I can't say."

I put my arm around her. Dari came and sat on the other side of the bench and held her hand. My grandmother had buried a husband she deeply loved and recited the words of farewell at the funeral of her only child, my mother. When my own son died and I had wanted to follow him into death, she had been there for me to guide me out of the grief. This woman had known pain in her life.

"Deirdre," my grandmother said, "are you sure you want to know what's in that scroll? It may be more than you can bear."

I looked at the case on the table and wondered. Maybe some stories shouldn't be told. But I had to know what it said. "Yes. I'm sure."

"Then begin now," she said. "I'm not going to sleep tonight and I doubt you or Dari will either. I'll light every lamp I have. A task you fear is best started right away."

We rose from the bench and went to work. Grandmother lit several tallow lamps from the hearth fire and placed them in a semicircle on the end of the dining table. Dari took the parchment I had given her out of her satchel and sat across the table from me with a pot of ink and a goose quill, ready to write the words I translated. When all was ready, I gently took the scroll out of the case and carefully unrolled the papyrus a few inches with my right hand, holding the rest of the scroll on the table with my left.

I began to read.

Chapter Four

T hese are the words of Miryam, mother of Yeshua of Nazareth, the one they call the Christ.

I never expected to grow old. I never wanted to. But the Almighty, blessed be his name, does not always give us what we want. So here I sit, an old woman, on a bench outside a hut in the village of Beth-horon near Jerusalem as the sun sets and young Rebekah writes down my words.

Yes, put your name on the scroll, Rebekah, and write down everything I say. After all, you're the one who wanted me to tell the story. You're also the one who worked so hard to learn to write, not me. I've never seen the point in writing—except of course the words of the Almighty and the prophets. They are worthy to be preserved and read for ages to come, mine are not. But stories—tales shared in the evening around the hearth fire—those I've always loved, even when I was a little girl, so long ago.

Rebekah wants to know how long ago it was. I know I was born in Nazareth in the hills of Galilee many years ago. It was late spring, just after the wheat harvest, and it was hot. My mother told me this. My father, who cared about such things, later told me I was born in the eighteenth year of the reign of King Herod—cursed be his name. How long ago was that, Rebekah? Eighty-nine years? That anyone should live so long!

My mother's mother told me many stories when I was a little girl. She practically raised me since my mother was always in the fields with my father trying to grow enough to feed our family and pay our taxes. When she was young, my grandmother was part of the war against Herod in Galilee. She and my grandfather joined the rebels led by Hezekiah and fought against Herod across the land. When Hezekiah and many of his men, including my grandfather, were captured and put to death without a trial before the Council of the Sanhedrin as was their right, my grandmother went to Jerusalem and joined the women who stood daily outside the temple demanding that Herod be brought to justice. They risked their lives doing this, but their voices grew so loud that Herod at last fled to the Romans at Damascus. My grandmother taught me that women can bend the will of kings if they stand together.

You want to know what my life was like when I was a girl, Rebekah? There isn't much to tell. I did the same things as every other girl in Galilee. I had one sister, also named Miryam, who was ten years older than me. She married a man named Clopas when I was very young. In our home growing up I had three brothers, so much of the household work fell to me. I woke up each morning before sunrise and helped my grandmother make the bread that was our main meal each day. I worked in the fields with my family to grow barley and wheat. I picked olives in season and tended the sheep. In the evenings I worked the loom, weaving wool and flax for our clothing. When I was eight I proudly made the first tunic to go over my undershirt and tied it around my waist with a belt of blue ribbon. I felt like the queen of Egypt!

My father and brothers would go to the local synagogue every Shabbat to study the scriptures. In those days it was just a dusty room in the back of a large house owned by an old widow named Rachel who paid for its upkeep and sponsored the rabbi, a part-time carpenter, whose son I would later marry. Sometimes my brothers and father would study with one of the Perushim, the Pharisees, who passed through Nazareth.

Did I learn to read? Rebekah, what a question! I was a girl. I couldn't study at the synagogue. I learned how to cook, weave, and take care of the young children. I helped my mother light the Shabbat candles. But I did listen every evening when my father and brothers talked about the law that the Almighty gave to Moshe on the mountain. I learned more than they ever thought I did, certainly more than a girl was supposed to know. Later, when we were married, Yosef taught me to read a little, though I was never very good at it. But I knew how to listen.

"She sounds," said my grandmother, "like a sensible woman. I've never seen the point of your Christian obsession with writing everything down. You must have learned it from the Jews. We druids never write down anything. It ruins the memory."

"Yes, Grandmother, I know. I'm a druid too, remember? Let me continue, please."

"Fine, child. Go ahead."

My grandmother's favorite story was the tale of Esther. She would tell it to me any time I would ask. You know the story, Rebekah. One night the Persian king Ahasuerus became drunk at a banquet and ordered his wife, Queen Vashti, to appear before him and his guests naked to display her beauty. Now Vashti was a proper lady and refused such a crude command. The king was furious and divorced her for disobedience, fearing she would set a bad example for wives throughout his kingdom. Ahasuerus then held a contest to find the most beautiful virgin in the land to become his new wife. He chose Esther, a Jewish maiden of the exile raised by her elderly cousin Mordecai, an important minister of the king who had once saved his life. After Esther married Ahasuerus, the evil Haman stirred up trouble and convinced the king that the Jews were a wicked people who should be exterminated. But Esther beseeched her people to fast and pray to the Almighty for deliverance. She then invited the king to a banquet and convinced him to spare the Jews.

When I was a girl, I would often imagine that I was Esther. In those rare moments when we had nothing to do, my girlfriends and I would pretend we were in the Persian court. I would invite the king to dine as I pleaded with him and used my beauty to win his favor. I was quite pretty in those days, by the way.

But girlhood doesn't last forever. By the time I was twelve, most of my friends had been betrothed to a husband, though of course they wouldn't be married until they had begun to menstruate. Many of these men were much older than my friends and were often widowers with children looking for a new wife to replace one who had died in childbirth. Having babies is a dangerous business. Two of my best friends died during labor within a few years of marriage. I held their hands as the blood gushed from their wombs and their eyes closed for the last time.

We all knew the dangers, but still we wanted to be mothers. I had held my little cousins and neighbor children in my arms since I was a child myself and pretended I was a mother with my own baby. I sang songs to them and changed their rags when they soiled themselves. I wanted to have a little one of my own more than anything.

Rebekah wants to know about Yosef. All right, I'll tell you.

One day just before my thirteenth birthday, my father told me he had found me a husband.

He said it was a fine match and that he had negotiated a favorable ketubah, or marriage contract, with the young man's father. I was thrilled when he said it was Yosef, the rabbi's son. I had known him since I was a little girl. He was tall and handsome with powerful arms and dark red hair. He was a distant cousin on my father's side only three years older than me. He lived with his family on the far side of the village near the road to Sepphoris. My father said he was a promising young carpenter, which I knew was true. Yosef had carved a doll for me as a gift years earlier when I was no more than six. He gave it to me one day while we were sitting with our families under a large olive tree in the fields just beyond the village. It was a small but beautiful figure of a woman in a fine flowing robe with a large headdress. I gave him a kiss on the cheek when no one was looking and slept with the doll every night. I still have it in the chest in my room.

My dowry was not large, just a few clothes, two hens, and three goats that I would bring with me to Yosef's home when we married. His family in turn promised to set aside a bride price of equal value that I would receive if he died before our children had grown, if he divorced me without cause, or if he lay with another woman.

Needless to say, I would forfeit my bride price and likely my life if I were unfaithful to him.

The wedding was still three months away when the messenger of the Almighty came to me. I was alone in my family's house. I don't know what I thought such a being would look like. I suppose like the seraphim with six wings in the writings of the prophets. But this messenger looked like a soldier from the days of my grandfather's grandfather. He was a young man with dark hair and a beard. He wore a leather breastplate over a blue tunic and bronze greaves above the dusty sandals on his feet. He had a short sword on his belt. He looked exhausted, like he had just come from battle. I might have thought he was a Roman except for the beard and his smell. It was sweet and unworldly. I was terrified. I knew immediately this was no mortal man. I fell to my knees and covered my face with my hands.

He spoke to me and told me not to be afraid. He said that I was blessed. He told me that the Almighty had made me pregnant and that I would give birth to a son named Yeshua, who would reign over his people forever. I raised my face and looked at him in terror. I said that was impossible, since I was a virgin. He then laughed, not unkindly, and told me that for the Almighty, nothing was impossible. I bowed my head and said I was the servant of the Almighty. Then I fainted.

When I woke, the messenger was gone. I was sure it had been a dream, but a month later I knew that I was pregnant. I was barely thirteen and unmarried. I had never been with a man. My life was ruined. How would I tell my parents? How would I tell Yosef?

I went to Yosef first. He was working in his father's shop alone building a table. I hoped he might believe me if I told him about the messenger from the Almighty. He did not. He stood there staring at me with a terrible look of pain and betrayal on his face. I left him and went back to my home, not knowing what to do. I thought about running away, but a young woman alone wandering the roads of Galilee would soon be dead or worse. So the next morning I told my parents. They were furious. My father cursed me and struck me with his fists. My mother spat in my face. I cowered, weeping and praying, as they screamed at me.

Soon their shouting and the reason for the turmoil had spread throughout the village. A crowd began to gather outside our house. Yosef's parents arrived and demanded I be brought forth. My own brothers dragged me out of the house into the town square and threw me at their feet by the village well. Yosef's father grabbed me by the hair and began cutting it off. Several men came forth and tore off my clothes so that I lay in the dust naked in front of the whole village. Everyone was yelling at me and cursing me. Then they began to pick up stones.

I knew then that I was going to die.

But suddenly there was a shout from the back of the crowd. Yosef pushed his way forward and knelt beside me. He took off his own cloak and covered me with it, then picked me up in his arms and carried me away while I clung to him. His family was shouting at him along with the rest of the people of Nazareth, who by then were thirsty for blood. He ignored them all and didn't stop until he reached the olive tree beyond the village where we had played as children. We were alone then. He lay me down gently on the ground as I still clung to him, weeping. He had a satchel on his back with a jug of water, bread, and some of his sisters' clothes. He gave them to me and turned his back while I dressed. He told me not to worry. We were leaving Nazareth that night and going away to raise our child.

I knew at that moment what it meant for someone to love me, really love me. I still thank the Almighty every day that he sent me a man like Yosef.

When the sun had set, we left the only place either of us had ever called home. I didn't know where we were going or when we would return, but I knew we would be together.

Chapter Five

The next morning before dawn, Dari and I gathered our things and left my grandmother's house. I didn't tell her where we were going nor did she ask. Just in case anyone was tracking us, we set off down the westward trail to the Barrow River. When we reached the stream in the middle of the day, we traveled south along the banks for a few hours, then crossed a ford as if we were heading to Kildare's daughter monastery at Sleaty. But after a mile or so we turned east again and recrossed the Barrow at a swift narrows while I held the satchel with the scroll high above my head, praying the whole time that I didn't drop it in the water.

We made camp in a dense thicket of birch trees and took off our wet clothes to hang on some bushes. I thought about building a small fire to dry them faster and ward off the chill of the evening, but decided against it for fear it might draw attention. A gentle wind made the golden birch leaves dance above us.

Dari and I wrapped ourselves in our wool blankets and huddled together for warmth. We had traveled a long way since morning and neither of us had slept for almost two days. With the satchel under my arm and my father's sword next to me, we fell asleep as soon as our heads touched the ground.

The next morning we softly sang one of the psalms and prayed, then quickly ate some bread and set off across the forest to the east. Dari had been unusually quiet during the previous day. I could tell she had been deep in thought.

"Deirdre, where are we going?"

"Glendalough. We need a safe, out-of-the-way place to work. I know Cormac will protect us there."

She raised her eyebrows at me with a hint of a smile.

Cormac was the king of his small tribe in the valley of Glendalough—the glen of the two lakes—deep in the heart of the Wicklow Mountains. He was also the first man I had ever loved.

It had been fifteen years earlier when we were both students at the monastery school at Kildare. I finally worked up the courage one night to sneak out of the girls' sleeping hut and meet him underneath a tree outside the monastery walls. I had never been with a boy before, but I think he realized that. He was gentle and thoughtful in every way a girl could wish for that night and all the others we slept together beneath that tree, wrapped together in a single blanket. I was heartbroken when he left the school to help his ailing father rule his kingdom, but I knew he had responsibilities at home.

"I'm sure he'll be glad to protect you, but is it a good idea to go there? Didn't he get married recently? I heard his wife is pregnant."

"Yes, but that has nothing to do with me."

"I hope his wife sees it that way. Women sometimes object when their husband's former lover shows up at the doorstep and asks to stay awhile."

"I'm a nun, Dari. I'm no threat to her."

"Somehow I don't think she'll believe that."

We passed quickly through the oak forests well south of Kildare heading east to the Wicklow Mountains in the distance.

"Deirdre, what do you think about the gospel? Do you think Mary really wrote it?"

We were walking uphill on a little-used path beneath the trees. A small thrush took offense at our intrusion and began singing *chip-chip-chip* in the branches above us.

"I don't know. I want to read more before I make up my mind."

"But it sounds right, like something I imagine Mary would say. It sounds like a woman talking, not like the Gospels composed by men that we have in the Bible."

"I'll admit that it sounds convincing. The author seems to be writing from the heart and doesn't contradict anything in the scriptures, but that could be the mark of a good forger. Father Ailbe has an old Greek scroll in in his chest that claims to have been written by a twin brother of Jesus named Thomas. It's full of secret teachings that Jesus supposedly revealed to Thomas during his ministry. Some of the teachings sound a lot like the sayings of Jesus in the Gospels, but some are very different. Father Ailbe says it was composed by the Gnostics decades after Jesus lived. I believe him. When you read the whole scroll through, it just doesn't feel right."

"And how does our scroll *feel* to you?"

"I don't know yet. Ask me when I finish translating it."

We walked another mile or so, then stopped to eat some bread and cheese in the tall grass on top of a barren hill. I looked back along our path and at the countryside all around but saw no signs of anyone. Still, I couldn't shake the feeling that we were being followed.

"Deirdre, I don't know Aramaic or much about Jewish customs, but when Mary—or whoever wrote the scroll—talks about Joseph, it sounds to me like a woman in love. And Joseph sounds like a real person. I always pictured him as a saintly older man leading Mary around on a donkey. This Joseph is a teenager who loved Mary from the time they were children. He had every reason to be furious at Mary when he found out she was pregnant. If I were him, I wouldn't have believed that she was visited by an angel. He could have stood by while she was stoned to death by the whole village. But he gave up everything for her."

"Yes, he sounds like a good man."

"I don't know. Maybe I just want to believe the story. Maybe it's because I wish I'd met a man like that instead of the brute I married."

It wasn't like Dari to talk about her past, even with me. She had told me only sparingly about how she had been raised by an abusive father on a poor farm and sold in marriage to a pig farmer who beat her regularly and almost killed her when he realized she couldn't have children. She let him freeze to death one night when he fell down a well in a drunken stupor. After that she became a nun to seek a better life.

"I know what you mean, Dari. The man I married was a bastard too. But at least he gave me a son, for a little while."

She put her arm around me. "My dear, we both deserved better. You could have married Cormac, you know. It wasn't more than a year ago that he proposed to you."

I sighed and pushed the hair out of my eyes. "Yes, I remember. I could have been Queen of Glendalough. But instead I chose to stay at a struggling monastery and become a celibate nun and fugitive scroll-translator."

Dari laughed. "Do you think Cormac's new wife knows about you and him?"

"I imagine so. Everyone else on this island seems to. And besides, as clever as Cormac is, no man can keep a secret from a woman."

It was late afternoon and rain clouds were gathering in the west. I felt exposed as we moved through the open grasslands south of Dún Ailinne, the ancient Leinster fort near the Liffey River to the north. Soon King Dúnlaing and his warriors would gather there for the annual Samain festival on the night our mortal world and the Otherworld of the spirits came closest together. I would have liked to have attended the feast to sing for them as a bard of the tribe, but I had a feeling I would be busy this year.

I pushed Dari on in the darkness into the foothills of the mountains beneath the high pass at the Wicklow Gap. We made a cold camp again in the forest by a small stream and ate what little was left of our bread and cheese.

We were up again before sunrise and over the pass through the mountains just as the first rays struck the gray boulders and fields of purple heather there. It began to rain as we followed a stream on the far side down the valley for several miles. Finally we left the trail and turned south over a rocky ridge until at last we looked down on the valley of Glendalough.

The two lakes far below looked like dark blue mirrors reflecting the storm clouds above us. The upper lake, beneath the steep round hills covered with oak and pine, was narrow but almost a mile long. The lower lake was smaller but no less striking. When Cormac had proposed to me, I was tempted to say yes if for no other reason than I could live here. It was easily the most beautiful place in Ireland.

Dari and I made our way down the ridge to the smaller lake where Cormac's settlement was. There were no towns or cities on our island such as Father Ailbe talked about across the sea in Britain and the rest of the old Roman Empire. Almost everyone in Ireland lived on a farm with their extended families and slaves, if they had any. Most settlements were no more than a few thatch-covered huts with space for maybe a dozen people and their animals. All were surrounded by low wooden or stone walls built more to keep the animals inside at night than repel invaders.

But kings like Cormac had larger farms with many huts, including an enormous feasting hall for entertaining his warriors and visitors, as well as conducting tribal business.

The guards at the gate bowed to me as a bard of the highest rank and told me the king was in the feasting hall conducting a hearing. Dari and I walked through the yard and were greeted respectfully by a number of men and women busy with preparations for harvest. The door to the feasting hall was open, so we entered.

The interior was dark, but a large fire blazed in the central hearth surrounded by wooden benches. The walls were hung with weapons and trophies from battle, including a few preserved heads of enemies slain by the king and his ancestors. Cormac himself was in his seat at the front of the hall before a small woman in her early twenties and a heavyset man about the same age standing next to her. The woman was gesturing and pointing at the man, who looked thoroughly miserable. Two old Brehon judges were seated on either side of the royal chair ready to give their advice and opinions when called on.

Cormac looked up when we entered the hall and seemed pleased, though surprised, to see me. He held up his hand to silence the complaining woman in front of him and got out of his chair to come and greet me.

"Deirdre," he said as he gave me a warm embrace, "this is an unexpected treat. It's so good to see you."

Cormac was as handsome as ever with easily the most charming smile I had ever seen on a man. His hair was long and blond, as was the bushy warrior's moustache on his otherwise clean-shaven face. He was not especially tall, but the powerful muscles beneath his tunic along with the confidence of his bearing made him seem a natural in his role as king, and also a leader of men in war. He wore a long crimson cloak embroidered in gold thread that must have cost him a fortune.

"And Dari," he said as he clasped her hands, "welcome back to my humble hall. Are you both all right?"

"Yes, thank you, Cormac," I answered. "There is an important matter we need to discuss with you, but it can wait until you're done here."

He nodded. "This won't take long," he said. "Simple divorce proceedings. I'll have one of my servants bring you some wine while you wait."

He clapped his hands and whispered to the slave who came running. She nodded and went to fetch the wine while we sat on one of the benches in back.

Cormac returned to his chair by the fire and motioned for the woman to continue.

"As I was saying, my lord, he just can't get the job done anymore. He's not a bad man, don't get me wrong, and I bear him no ill, but I've only got two children, both daughters, and no sons. My husband loves his ale and eats more porridge every morning than any man I know. He works hard enough in our fields every day, but he keeps getting fatter every year. It's gotten to where he can't even do his business when we go to bed at night. It's not his weight—I don't mind being on top, mind you—but he's as limp as a wet rag. Why the other night he couldn't even—"

Cormac held up his hand to the woman again. "Yes, Tethba, I believe I understand." He turned to the man. "Luchtar, do you have anything to say in your defense?"

The poor fellow looked up and started to open his mouth, then shook his head.

Cormac conferred for a moment with the two Brehon judges, then addressed the couple. "Luchtar son of Nuadu and Tethba daughter of Saingliu, it is always a tragedy when a marriage fails. We hope for love and support from our spouses, but the primary purpose of marriage nonetheless is the bearing and raising of children. Luchtar, I am sorry. You are a good husband and provider for your family, but if you can no longer get your wife pregnant, she has ample grounds to divorce you. I rule this marriage dissolved. The Brehons will work out the details of property distribution and the return of the dowry. You are both free to remarry as you wish. But Luchtar, know that as in all marriages, you will be responsible for the upkeep of your daughters by Tethba until they are married."

Cormac clapped his hands and two guards entered the hall. They escorted the Brehons outside with the now-divorced couple following behind. The king called for food and drink, then motioned us both to benches close to the fire. Servants appeared with a small jar of Gaulish wine, silver cups, and a plate of pork loin with a large loaf of fresh bread and butter.

Cormac could tell we were famished, so he graciously let us eat our fill while he told us the latest news about mutual friends. When we were done, the slaves appeared and took away our dishes after bringing us another jar of excellent wine.

"Now," said Cormac, "how can I help you?"

I told him everything, beginning with the arrival of Sister Branwen at Kildare. He listened carefully, nodding a few times when I described the threat the scroll posed to the monastery. When I was finished, he poured the three of us another cup of wine.

"You have a problem, Deirdre."

"Yes, Cormac, I know."

"Are you sure this scroll is worth the trouble? You could hand it over to whoever is searching for it and be done with the whole matter. You could even negotiate some benefits for the monastery in exchange for surrendering it."

"It crossed my mind, believe me. But this scroll is important. If I finish translating it and decide that it's a fake, I'll gladly turn it over to them. I don't have any desire to have another false gospel in circulation. That would be bad for the whole church and bring down the full wrath of the bishops and Rome on Kildare.

But it's come into my care and I need to know if it's genuine. If Mary really told this story, then it's an incredibly important look at the life of Jesus and the early church. Matthew, Mark, Luke, John, Paul—they were all good *men*, but men. We don't have anything written by a woman, let alone the mother of Christ himself."

"I understand," said Cormac. "I really do. I'm no believer in your Christian god or divine providence, but even I am impressed that this scroll has miraculously survived the centuries to be delivered to you. And I certainly wouldn't mind seeing the church hierarchy taken down a few notches. But you're playing a dangerous game with some very powerful people. This could turn out badly for you and the monastery at Kildare. Call me sentimental for my school days, but I don't want to see all that Brigid and Sister Anna and Father Ailbe have worked for destroyed. And even more than that, I don't want to see you hurt. The men seeking this scroll may be Christians, but they won't hesitate to kill you to get it." He reached out his hand and held mine. "Think about it, Deirdre. I care about what happens to you. I'll act as your intermediary if you want and work out a good deal for Kildare with the bishops and Rome."

At that moment I heard a woman's voice from the back of the hall. "Well, my dear, I see we have guests."

Cormac quickly dropped my hand and stood up to face the door. Dari and I stood as well.

The woman who had just entered was beautiful. She was wearing a dark green cloak and had long golden hair that flowed over her shoulders in intricate braids. I could see her bright blue eyes even in the dimness of the feasting hall. She had a face that Helen of Troy would have envied. She was also very pregnant.

"Sisters Deirdre and Dari," Cormac said with his most charming smile, "I would like to present my wife, Áine, daughter of King Eógan of the Uí Chiennselaig tribe."

Cormac walked quickly to the door and led her back to the fire to join us. Dari and I both bowed as Cormac settled her onto a bench next to him. He was the image of a devoted husband as he made sure she was comfortable and poured her a cup of wine with his own hand.

"Please be seated, ladies," she said. "I'm glad to meet you, Sister Dari. And of course it's good to see you again, Deirdre."

I had met Áine a number of times over the years at festivals and gatherings around Leinster. She was perhaps ten years younger than me. Her father ruled a tribe on the coast farther south below the Wicklow Mountains. His port, where the Avoca River met the sea, was the most prosperous in Ireland. It controlled much of the trade with Britain and Gaul, as well as welcomed occasional merchant ships from Rome and Alexandria. Aside from her obvious beauty, Áine was a fine catch for Cormac because of her family's wealth and contacts with the world beyond our island. My old friend was nothing if not an ambitious man.

"My congratulations on your marriage, Áine," I said, "and on your expected child. May God prosper and bless you."

"Thank you, Deirdre. I was so sorry you couldn't attend the wedding. I suppose the duties of a nun are quite demanding."

Áine had indeed invited me to the wedding, but she had sent the messenger only the day before the ceremony with apologies that I had been overlooked in all the festivities.

"Yes, it was gracious of you to invite me, though."

"But of course. Any friend of Cormac's is a friend of mine as well."

She placed her hand on Cormac's and squeezed it, hard. He was looking distinctly uncomfortable.

"May I ask what brings you to our little kingdom?"

"Monastery business," I answered. "I'm translating an old scroll and was looking for a quiet place to work away from the bustle of Kildare."

I don't know why I didn't tell her the whole story. I knew she would get it all from Cormac when she was alone with him.

"Well, that would be lovely, wouldn't it, Cormac? Of course, with all the preparations for harvest I'm afraid there isn't much peace here. And there certainly isn't any room fit for such important guests. But I know my father would be happy to take you in and provide suitable accommodations. I'll have one of our men escort you there. It's not far at all."

Cormac cleared his throat. "That really won't be necessary, my love."

I felt a sudden chill in the hall.

"Deirdre and Dari," he said, without meeting Áine's eyes, "can stay in the hut at Moccu's well near the upper lake. It's quiet there and the morning light is excellent for reading. I'll send food every day and post a guard to keep away anyone who might bother them."

She stared at him for a moment, then smiled. "Then it's all settled," she said. "I'll send one of my servants to make sure the hut is clean and has plenty of turf for the fire."

She stood up and we stood with her. "I hope you'll forgive me, Deirdre, but my back starts to ache whenever I sit anywhere too long. You were a mother once and must understand."

I swallowed hard. "Of course."

"I know you'll be busy working on your scroll," she said as she walked to the door, "but I hope we'll be able to visit together, just the two of us women."

"I look forward to it."

Dari and I both bowed as she left. Cormac sat down again on the bench across from us and poured himself a very large cup of wine.

"That went well," he said with a forced grin. "I'm sorry, Deirdre."

"I'm the one who should be sorry that I've made trouble for you."

"Áine and trouble go together hand in hand," he replied. "Don't get me wrong. She's a fine woman and an excellent queen, but she's got a mind of her own and a fierce sense of what belongs to her. She knows all about you and me. I don't think those robes of a nun that you wear will put her mind at ease. She's probably afraid I'm going to sneak off to Moccu's hut and visit you one night. She doesn't need to worry—not that it isn't tempting."

Dari told me later that I blushed as bright as a primrose at that point.

Thankfully, one of Cormac's guards appeared just then at the door of the feasting hall.

"My lord, you have a visitor."

"Who is it?" Cormac asked.

"A Christian monk. And he claims that he's come all the way from Rome."

Chapter Six

"Wait here," Cormac said to Dari and me as he stood up and put his royal robe around his shoulders. "I don't want him to know you're here. If he asks, I'll tell him I haven't seen you and have no idea where you are."

"It's too late for that," I said. "I don't think he would be here unless he knows we are too. Besides, I want to talk with him."

"Deirdre," he said, "that is a very bad idea. Let me deal with him. I'll send him packing back to Rome."

"You know that won't help. They'll just send someone else. Better I talk with him now and find out exactly what he wants."

Cormac shook his head. "Fine. But Dari, you remain here with the scroll."

Cormac gave orders to his guard to stay with Dari. I handed her the case, straightened my robes, and followed Cormac out the door.

The visitor was waiting in the center of the settlement by the well. He was a rather handsome man of average height with a fair complexion and a head of short gray hair. He must have been about forty years old, but he looked fit and strong, like a warrior. His face was kind and reminded me of Father Ailbe. He wore a gray traveling cloak over his homespun tunic and carried a large traveling satchel on his shoulder. He wore no sword or weapons on his belt, just a small wooden cross on a leather thong around his neck.

He bowed to us both as we approached. "King Cormac, Sister Deirdre, my name is Bartholomew. Thank you for seeing me. My lord, please forgive me for arriving in your kingdom unannounced and without escort. I realize it's against the custom of your land. I can only plead for your forgiveness because of the urgency of my task."

His Irish was quite good, with only a trace of an accent.

"And what would that task be, Father?" asked Cormac.

"Not Father, I'm afraid. I'm not an ordained priest, just a monk sent by Pope Hormisdas."

"And why would the pope send you all the way to our island?" I asked.

"To seek a document of great concern to the church."

Cormac looked up at the sky. "It seems we're going to get more rain. Let's go into my armory and discuss this."

Cormac led the two of us to a nearby hut where the tribe stored their weapons, mostly swords and short spears. A few preserved heads of slain enemies were hanging on the walls of this hut as well. A small turf fire was burning in the hearth. We sat down on benches near the fire facing one another. Cormac called one of his slaves to bring wine.

Bartholomew studied the weapons and heads on the walls as the slave filled our cups. He seemed neither shocked nor intimidated, if that had been Cormac's intention.

"Now, Brother Bartholomew, let me be quite clear. I have no quarrel with the church, but I will not allow any guest in my kingdom to be threatened in any way. If you have something to say to Sister Deirdre, say it, but be careful of your words."

"I would never threaten anyone, my lord, especially a sister of holy Brigid, for whom I have the greatest respect."

I was watching Bartholomew closely as he spoke. As a druid, I was trained to look beneath the surface of things and people. I had been expecting a wide-eyed fanatic threatening me with the fires of hell if I didn't hand over the scroll. This man had a gentle soul and a nimble, open mind.

"Cormac," I said, "would you mind if I spoke with Brother Bartholomew alone?"

Cormac frowned at me and hesitated for a moment, then nodded and rose. "Deirdre, I'll have two guards outside the door. Don't hesitate to call if you need them."

Cormac left the two of us alone in the hut. Bartholomew refilled my cup.

"This is excellent wine," he said. "From southern Gaul, isn't it? It reminds me of the vintage my father, God rest his soul, grew in Tuscany."

"You're Italian then?"

"Yes, my family lives on a small estate outside of Arretium in the hills south of the Arno River. My mother is there still with my sisters and their husbands."

"Tuscany is ruled by the Ostrogoths, isn't it," I asked, "along with most of Italy?"

"Yes, under the rule of Theodoric. He's a just king, even though he follows the Arian heresy along with most of his people. He's recently made peace with the pope and allows the native Romans to follow the Catholic faith openly and without interference."

"Father Ailbe told me about that. He often corresponds with his friends in Gaul and Italy, as well as Constantinople and Alexandria."

"Father Ailbe is well known and respected in Rome," Bartholomew said. "The pope himself has spoken of him to me most favorably."

"If that's true," I said, "why does Rome keep trying to shut down our monastery at Kildare?"

"That, Sister Deirdre, is an oversimplification. It would be more accurate to say that some factions in the Roman hierarchy do not support your work. Others, including the holy father and myself, are more open to your mission."

"Kind words, Brother Bartholomew, but I've learned to beware of men who try to beguile women with sweet talk before they make their true intentions known. Let's be honest with each other. Tell me first, how did you find me?"

"I followed you."

"From Kildare and my grandmother's house?"

"Yes."

"That's impressive. I've hunted in these lands since I was a little girl. I took precautions to make sure we didn't leave a trace."

"I've also hunted since I was a child. And I was a scout in the army of Theodoric."

"Don't you think that stalking someone through the woods and hills could be seen as the act of an enemy? Why didn't you just come to our campsite at night and slit our throats while we slept?"

He seemed genuinely pained by my words. Then again, maybe he was a very good actor. "Sister Deirdre,

I don't know what kind of man you think I am, but I do not murder women in their beds. I killed men when I was a soldier in the army. I'm not proud of it, but I did my duty to my king. Now I serve Christ and the church. I could have come to your camp and perhaps stolen the scroll I know you have, but I waited until you were in a safe place before I made myself known and came forward to talk with you. I prefer using reason to theft or violence."

"Did you follow Sister Branwen from Britain as well?"

"Not exactly. When I heard that a nun had secretly left the monastery where I suspected the scroll was hidden, I made my way to Ireland to see if I might find and talk with her. I heard from some farmers along the way that she was heading for Kildare. I didn't catch up with her until she was within sight of your monastery. I saw her fall and you come to her aid. I'm sorry to hear that she passed away. I'm sure she was a good woman."

"Did you talk to Father Ailbe and Sister Anna after we left?"

"No. I didn't want to put them in the position of lying to protect you, as I'm sure they would have. And before you ask, I didn't bother your grandmother either. I simply waited until you left her house that morning and tracked you on your roundabout journey until you came here to Glendalough."

"How did you learn our language?"

"From Irish slaves at the papal court. The holy father wanted me to learn the languages of these northern lands so that he could send me on diplomatic missions for the church. I also speak British and Saxon, along with Frankish and Burgundian. I've been to Ireland twice before. The pope sent me on two missions to Armagh to negotiate with the abbot. I spent several months there each time and learned a great deal about your island and its people. The abbot spoke of you, by the way."

"I bet he did. We've had some rather serious disagreements."

"Yes. He's not my favorite person either, but he's a powerful man with influential friends in Rome."

"Brother Bartholomew, what is it you want from me?"

He poured me another cup of wine before answering. "I think you already know. You have in your possession an ancient scroll that was supposedly composed by the Virgin Mary. The church authorities have been searching for it for almost five hundred years. It's a very dangerous document. I want to destroy it."

"You seem like a reasonable man, Bartholomew. I admit nothing regarding this scroll. But assuming I do have it, why would you want to destroy something that may have been written by the mother of Jesus? You don't even know what it says."

"No, I don't know what it says. I admit that if it's genuine, it would be fascinating to read. Even if it's a forgery, it would be interesting see what it contains."

"Then let me finish translating it—assuming I have it, that is. If it's clearly a fake, then I would turn it over to you and that would be the end. But if it's genuine, it could change everything."

"That, Deirdre, is why I must destroy it."

"You're afraid it's going to cause some sort of uproar in the church? A schism? A revolution among Christian women? Are you really that afraid of what Mary might have said?"

He stood up and stretched his arms. "These trips are getting harder on my bones as I grow older. Sometimes I wish I were back on my family's farm in Tuscany tending the grapevines and drinking wine under the Italian sun." He walked to the fire to warm his hands. "Deirdre, do you think I want to destroy this scroll because I hate women? That perhaps I'm some sort of twisted misogynist like the abbot of Armagh?"

"It crossed my mind," I answered.

"I was married once," he said. "She was a beautiful woman I had known since we were children. Her name was Priscilla. I was nineteen on our wedding day and she was sixteen. She was the love of my life. Two years later, she gave birth to a little girl we named Maria. I was a soldier then and was away often on campaigns with Theodoric in the north. But every time I left home I marked the days of my absence on a slate I kept in my pack so that I could know how long it was until I would see them again. There were plenty of prostitutes

I could have spent the night with like most of the men did. But all I wanted was to be with Priscilla and hold my little girl in my arms.

"Vandal raiders struck Tuscany when I was away one summer with Theodoric and the army. They burned my family's farm and killed my father. My mother and sisters escaped into the hills. They tried to save my wife and daughter, but it was too late. I came back a month later to find their graves beside the church in our village. I wish I could have died with them. Instead, I put aside my weapons and armor to become a monk and serve the church of Christ."

"I'm sorry, Bartholomew."

"Deirdre, I don't hate women. I don't want to destroy this scroll to silence your voices. And I certainly don't want keep you as lowly servants of priests and monks as the nuns are at Armagh. If it were up to me, women would have been equal with men from the beginning of the faith. I know that women are every bit as intelligent and capable as men, often more so. But it's not up to me. The church is what it is. To try and change things now would be disastrous."

"But why?" I asked. "Why would it be such a terrible thing to hear what Mary has to say? Maybe it's not dangerous at all. Maybe the church would go on as it always has. Maybe the scroll would just add a woman's voice to the chorus of those who wrote about Christ. Maybe it could make the church stronger."

He sat down again across from me. "We simply can't take that chance. You know what's happening in the world beyond this island. Britain is being overrun by pagan Saxons. Our churches there are being burned and the invaders sacrifice our priests to their gods Woden and Frige. Only in the west and north have the native British made a stand. And how long can they hold out? Across the channel the Franks under their late King Clovis accepted baptism, but their Christianity is political, not personal. I've seen Frankish lords take communion at mass in the morning and offer cattle on altars to their old gods that same afternoon. The Vandals, Visigoths, and Ostrogoths who rule in the west are not much better. The Christian emperor at Constantinople faces threats on every front, from the Huns to his north to the Persians and Arabs on his eastern border. And within Christianity the church is threatening to tear itself apart. It's not just heretics like the Arians, Pelagians, and Nestorians. There are a thousand different sects each claiming they are the true followers of Jesus. Some are harmless enough, but others question the foundations of Christian teaching, like the inspiration of scripture, the role of Christ in salvation, and even the truth of the resurrection."

"Yes, I know about all the threats to the church. But do you think the words of Mary, if that's whose they are, will make things worse? Maybe she could bring healing and new life to the faith."

"Deirdre, I wish it were that simple. If it were, I would shout her words from the rooftops. But you know the world doesn't work that way. Publish that gospel, whatever it says, even if it's genuine, and you will shatter the church like glass. We'll have a hundred new sects all claiming to be the true faith revealed to us by Christ through his mother. We can't allow that. The church is hanging on by a thread in this world. I honor and revere the mother of Christ, but I would rather see her words vanish in flames than tear the church apart."

I sat on the bench for several minutes watching the fire and thinking about what Bartholomew had said. All of his arguments made sense. Finally I closed my eyes and prayed. Then I stood up and clapped my hands. The guards entered at once.

"Take this man and give him food for his journey. Then escort him to the borders of your kingdom and see that he doesn't return."

Bartholomew sighed deeply and shook his head. "Please don't do this. I don't want to fight you. Please just give me the scroll."

"I'm sorry, Bartholomew. Yes, I have the scroll. Yes, I'm going to translate it. If I think it's genuine, I'm going to let the world know what it says. I have to believe it came into my hands for a reason. Generations of women have cherished it and given their lives to protect it. I cannot betray them and hand it over to you to be burned. I'm going to trust that God will see the matter accomplished according to his will."

Bartholomew picked up his satchel and put it across his shoulder. "You must understand that I have to stop you. Do you know what that means?"

"Yes, I do."

He moved in front of me. The guards drew their swords and held the points at his throat. I held up my hand to them.

Then Bartholomew kissed me gently on the cheek. "The peace of the Lord be with you, Deirdre."

"And also with you, Bartholomew."

Chapter Seven

Cormac settled us in Moccu's hut on the shores of Glendalough's upper lake. It was quite comfortable and had a window with excellent light for reading. There was a large bed for Dari and me in the corner and a hearth stocked with sweet-smelling turf for the fire. Cormac had given us plenty of food and a whole barrel of honeyed ale. He also posted not one but three very large guards around the hut at all hours.

I was saddened that Bartholomew and I had parted as we did. I had the feeling we could have been friends under different circumstances. What made it worse was that I understood his arguments for burning the scroll. It was possible that in this small hut in a peaceful valley in Ireland, I was setting in motion events that would tear the church apart. That was the last thing I wanted to do. Although I was a druid and respected the traditions of my people, I believed in the hope and promise that Christianity had brought to our island. I wanted the church to grow and prosper, not come crashing down because of me. I hoped that I was doing the right thing in the eyes of God, but I wasn't sure.

I wondered what Bartholomew was planning. I felt fairly safe at Glendalough, at least for the moment. I didn't think he would attack us directly there. The borders of the small kingdom were well guarded and Cormac had earned a reputation as a fierce and tireless warrior. His men were loyal to a fault and would lay down their lives to protect us as guests of their king. My best guess was that Bartholomew would retreat for the time being and lay his plans for stopping us. He didn't like the abbot at Armagh, but that wicked little man was his natural ally in this fight. The abbot was not only an enemy of Brigid and our work at Kildare, but he was a son of the powerful Uí Néill dynasty of Ulster in the north, the sworn foes of my people in Leinster. He hated me, the monastery of Brigid, and women in general—in that order. I had humiliated him a year earlier when I traveled to Armagh in search of the stolen bones of holy Brigid only to leave him bound and gagged facedown in his hut when he tried to kill me. He would leap at the chance for revenge against me and to curry favor with Rome by destroying the scroll. Bartholomew would certainly use him, even if reluctantly, but a direct attack on Glendalough was an unlikely tactic. More likely Bartholomew would hire outlaws to sneak into the valley and steal the scroll. The bandits of Ireland were very good at their job and could be bought for the right price—money which I was sure the abbot would provide from his plentiful treasury. I didn't think Bartholomew wanted to harm me or Dari if it could be avoided, but I had no doubt that if he thought it was necessary, he wouldn't hesitate to have us killed.

The next morning as soon as the sun rose Dari and I sat at the table under the window. I pulled the scroll carefully from its case and unrolled the papyrus so that I could read the next section. After a brief prayer, I began to translate:

> It was five years before Yosef and I returned to Nazareth to live. A plague had swept across Galilee during our absence and killed half the people in our village, including both of his parents and my father.
>
> Rebekah says I'm skipping ahead. She wants to know about the birth of Yeshua. Fine, child, I'll tell you.

You thought perhaps it was miraculous and free from pain? I wish it had been! I gave birth to my son alone in a barn we were living in with only Yosef there to help me. The poor man was even more terrified than I was. The labor was long and painful beyond anything I had known in my young life. But when it was over, Yosef wrapped little Yeshua in an old blanket and handed him to me.

I had never seen such a beautiful child. I suppose every mother feels that way about her baby, but I think it was true. When he was only a few minutes old he opened his eyes and looked at me, really looked at me. I had never seen a newborn do that before. Then he started to cry like any other baby. I put him to my breast for the first time. He was calm as he nursed and looked up at me the whole time. I knew then I would never love anyone like I loved this child.

Yosef circumcised him in front of our barn on the eighth day after he was born. His hands were shaking as he held the knife, but he did a fine job. When I had wrapped soft cloth around the wound to stop the bleeding, Yosef lifted him up to heaven and declared that this was Yeshua, his son. He was now the legitimate heir of Yosef the carpenter of Nazareth. Whatever had happened before, no one could question now that my Yeshua was a member of the house of Yisrael. Or at least that was the law. If we had been at home, my mother and aunts might have invited the whole village to a celebration with a table spread with fruit, wheat cakes, and even a roasted lamb. But we were alone. We ate some olives and cold barley porridge, then went to bed.

Before we returned to Nazareth we moved around to several different villages, wherever Yosef could find employment. He was a hard worker and excellent craftsman, but he sometimes had trouble finding a job for the day, even laboring in the fields. There were many poor farmers and their families wandering the roads who had lost their lands to the tax collectors. The Romans had tried to take a census to squeeze even more money out of the Jews, but Zadok the Pharisee led a resistance against them, preaching that the land belonged to the Almighty, not the Romans. In the end, the Jews lost and the Romans won. They always do.

We lived for a while in the small village of Bethlehem only a few miles from Nazareth.

"Wait a minute," Dari interrupted. "Are you sure you read that right? You said Bethlehem was near Nazareth. I thought Jesus was born far from there, near Jerusalem."

"Yes, Dari, I translated it right. The scroll says it was near Nazareth. But there are two Bethlehems in the Bible, one in Judea and another in Galilee. The book of Joshua talks about this Bethlehem of Galilee. But Mary doesn't say that Jesus was born in Galilee, just that they were living there when he was a toddler. There's a lot about the life of Jesus we don't know."

"But where are the wise men from the east and the shepherds? Mary doesn't talk about them. Does that mean those stories didn't really happen? Or that this scroll is a forgery?"

"Neither. Mary isn't writing a biography. None of the Gospel authors were. They're telling the parts of the life of Jesus that fit into their particular story. The Gospels of Mark and John in the Bible don't talk about the birth of Jesus at all. It seems in this gospel that Mary wants to tell the story of Jesus from a mother's point of view. She may leave out a lot of things we're familiar with."

"You sound like you've already decided Mary did write this."

"I didn't say that. Now may I continue?"

"Yes."

We lived for a while in the small village of Bethlehem only a few miles from Nazareth. It was when Yosef's parents and my father were still alive. Yeshua was not quite a year old then and was finally sleeping through the night. We walked all the way to Nazareth one Shabbat morning. I stood outside the house of Yosef's family holding Yeshua while he spoke with his father inside. There was shouting and cursing. Yosef came out, shook his head, and led me away. We walked around to the far side of the village where my family lived. Yosef went inside, but the reception was the same. Then as we were leaving, my grandmother came out of the house. She could barely walk even with the olivewood cane she used. Her eyes lit up with joy as she embraced me. She held Yeshua in her arms and kissed him, then lay her hand on him and blessed him. She kissed me a final time and told me that she would always love me. I could barely see her through my tears. Then she hobbled back into the house. I heard the next month that she had died in her sleep.

What do I remember about Yeshua as a child? What sort of stories would you like, Rebekah? Do you imagine he called down rain from the skies or parted the waters of the Red Sea like Moshe? But there was no water in Nazareth aside from what we drew from the well and a small creek that flowed for a few hours after a heavy storm.

Let me tell you a story.

We had just moved back to Nazareth. Most of the people who had known us were dead and there were many new settlers in town who were refugees from the fighting after the death of Herod. Most of my friends who were still alive were so glad to have someone they knew to talk to that they didn't care about what had happened five years earlier. Some of the older women in town wouldn't speak to me and several spat at my feet for years whenever I walked by, but most people were happy to have a young couple with a child back in town since so many little ones had died.

Yeshua was playing with some boys one Shabbat afternoon in the creek after a spring rain. They were piling up rocks to make pools in the stream and splashing about as boys will. After a while, Yeshua started to shape little sparrows out of the mud. Yosef was sitting under a shade tree nearby with his friend Annas, the town scribe. Annas said that Yosef shouldn't let his son profane Shabbat by laboring with his hands, so Yosef called to him to stop. But Yeshua pretended not to hear and kept making birds. Yosef got up and went to him and told him that it was not right to make mud animals on the day of rest. Yeshua looked up at him and said that they weren't mud, they were alive. Then

Yeshua stood up and clapped his hands, shouting to the sparrows to fly away. Yosef told me later that for a moment he actually wondered if they would. But of course they were nothing but mud creatures made by a little boy. When Yeshua saw that they weren't alive, he started to cry and Yosef carried him home.

Yeshua was always a most compassionate child. There was a little girl in our village named Sarah a few years younger than him who was deformed from birth. She had slanted eyes, a flattened face, and was slow to grow and learn. Children like Sarah were usually left to die at birth, though the rabbis taught that all life was a gift from the Almighty. But Sarah's mother had no other children. After many miscarriages, she at last gave birth to Sarah when she was past forty and had almost given up hope for ever having a child. The midwife and even her husband urged her to let them quietly leave the girl in an old well outside the village, but she would not listen to them. The people of the town shook their heads and went on with their lives.

The children in Nazareth wouldn't play with Sarah, even though she was a sweet girl who always had a bright smile for everyone. Sometimes the boys would throw rocks at her. Most of the time she stayed inside her home with her mother.

From the time Sarah was old enough to sit up, Yeshua alone would play with her. They lived only two houses away from us, so often he would go and sit with her, telling her stories or making toys for her with sticks and old pieces of wood from Yosef's workshop. His mother told me many times in tears how grateful she was to my son for being a friend to Sarah when no one else would.

One day when he was about eight, I finally asked Yeshua why he played with Sarah.

"I don't understand, Mother," he answered. He was eating bread at the table as we talked and trying to repair a broken toy horse that had lost the bottom of one leg.

"I mean, Yeshua, that Sarah, as nice as she is, is not like other children. She's slow to learn and can barely talk. I think it's very kind of you to play with her, but wouldn't you rather be with your other friends?"

"I play with the boys of the town all the time," he said. He was having no luck fixing the leg. The horse would barely stand.

"Yes, Yeshua, but Sarah isn't going to get better no matter how much time you spend with her. She's never going to be normal."

He put the horse down and looked at me curiously.

"I don't play with her to make her better, Mother. I play with her because she's my friend. Don't you think she matters as much as everyone else?"

"Yes, Yeshua, I'm sure the Almighty loves her as much as anyone."

He took a bite of bread and seemed thoughtful for a minute.

"I know what people think of her, Mother. I know they think she's slow and should have been left to die as a baby. I hear people talk, you know. But people are wrong. Do you think that when the Almighty looks at the people of this world, he sees Sarah any differently than the rest of us? He must be so much greater than us that we all seem broken to him, like this horse. But it doesn't mean we should be thrown away, even if we can't be fixed."

He finished his bread and took the horse outside to play with some of his other toys in front of our house under the morning shade of a tamarisk tree.

You want another story about Yeshua, Rebekah? Do you think perhaps he raised the dead as a boy? Then listen. A few years later Yeshua was playing with his best friend, a Greek boy named Zenon.

Normally Jews and Greeks kept to themselves and no Greeks lived in Nazareth, but Zenon's father was a carpenter who often worked with Yosef in Sepphoris just a few miles away. Times were hard and my husband, like most men in Galilee, took whatever job he could find. Yeshua would often go to Sepphoris to help Yosef and they would stay several days at a time in the home of an old Jewish widow on the edge of the town. Zenon and his family lived next to the widow. He was the same age as Yeshua and a fine boy, for one of the goyim. At first neither child could understand the other, but as children will, they played together anyway. In less than a year, Yeshua was speaking Greek like a native and Zenon spoke our language just as well.

It happened one warm evening that he and Zenon were playing on the flat roof of Zenon's house. They were running about when Zenon tripped and fell off the roof onto the hard ground below. Yosef and Zenon's parents were sitting on the roof when it happened, enjoying the cool breeze after sunset. They and Yeshua rushed to the ground where Zenon lay, but there was nothing anyone could do. His mother was beside herself with grief and screamed at Yeshua, blaming him for her son's death. But my son didn't even hear her. He was holding Zenon

*in his arms and telling his friend to get up.
But Zenon was gone and nothing my son could
say would bring him back. It was that day that
Yeshua learned what death is.*

*I'm sorry, Rebekah. You'll think all my sto-
ries of Yeshua are sad. Far from it. He was a
happy child and always obeyed his parents—at
least most of the time. He was a boy after all.
Watching him grow was the greatest joy of my
life. Even my mother in time welcomed us back
into my family home if for no other reason than
she could be with her grandson.*

*You want to know if there was anything dif-
ferent about Yeshua as a boy, anything that
might show what he was to become? You may
be surprised at the answer, which is no. I always
thought he was remarkable, but every mother
thinks that of her child. But Yeshua as a boy
worked no miracles, healed no one who was
sick, and certainly never raised anyone from
the dead.*

*He was an exceptional student though.
Before he was six years old, he had already
learned how to read from Yosef. I remember
watching them proudly in the evenings as they
sat together and read the old scrolls Yosef had
received from his father. The plague had killed
many of the men of Nazareth so that there were*

few left who could read the Torah well and lead Shabbat services. Yosef, as the son of the village rabbi, became a part-time rabbi himself. The woman who had sponsored our synagogue in her home had died in the plague and her house was sold, so Yosef's workshop became our new synagogue and house of prayer. It wasn't much to look at, just a few tables brushed clear of sawdust and a wooden chest in the corner for our Torah and the other scrolls. On Shabbat the men would gather there for scripture readings, prayers, hymns, and sermons, with the women standing in the back. It also served as our Bet ha-Sefer where the boys learned to read and study the scriptures. Whenever he wasn't working or playing with his friends, Yeshua would be there studying the scrolls, with Yosef or by himself, sometimes late into the night by the light of a flickering lamp.

I remember one day when he was thirteen he came to me with a question. Yosef was away for the day on some job that didn't require any help. Yeshua had been studying a scroll of his favorite prophet Yesha'yahu, the one the Greeks call Isaiah. When the two of us sat down to our evening meal, he asked me:

"Mother, do you remember what Yesha'yahu said when he stood before the presence of the

Almighty in a vision and one of the seraphim touched his lips with a burning coal to purify him?"

"Yes, my boy. The Almighty asked who would go for him to preach to his people and Yesha'yahu said, 'Here am I, send me.'"

"But mother, then the Almighty told the prophet that he should preach to his people even though they wouldn't listen, even though through their unbelief their home would become a wasteland. Why would the Almighty tell him to do that? Why preach to a people if they won't listen?"

"I don't know, my son. Maybe the preaching is more important than the listening. Perhaps proclaiming the words of the Almighty is a blessing in itself."

Yeshua closed his eyes then as he often did when he was thinking.

"No, Mother, I don't think that's it."

"You tell me then, Yeshua."

"I think the Almighty wanted us to learn something. I think he wanted us to learn that spreading his word is like sowing seeds of grain in rocky soil. Most of it will not bear fruit. Some will be eaten by birds. Some of it will wash away in the winter rains. But it will always happen that a few seeds will find good soil and grow. I think the Almighty wanted us to learn that there is always fruit that will grow, even when it seems no one is listening."

I put my hand on his cheek.

"You may be right, my son. You may be right."

And so, Rebekah, our life went on happily for many years. I would rise each morning before dawn to fetch water from the well, then make our bread for the day. After this I would wake up Yosef and Yeshua, who was always sleepy in the mornings, and we would eat and pray before they went to work in the shop or wherever the job was that day. I would take care of our house, draw water, tend the garden, grind grain, weave our clothes, maybe visit with friends, and wait for my men to finish their labor. Every harvest the whole village was in the fields until long after sunset. It was a hard life, but a good one. Yeshua grew into a fine young man. Sometimes months would go by without me thinking of the messenger of the Almighty who had come to me years before. I began to dream that Yeshua would someday marry a nice girl, have many children, take over the workshop from Yosef, and become our village rabbi. Yosef and I would grow old together surrounded by grandchildren and cared for by a loving son. I had many dreams. But then everything changed forever.

Chapter Eight

Deirdre, it's getting dark. I'd love to go on, but I can barely see what I'm writing and I don't want to make mistakes. Do you want to light some candles and keep going?"

"No, let's stop for the night. I can't see the scroll clearly myself. And I'm getting hungry."

I slowly rolled up the scroll and put it back in its case, then put it under my pillow on the bed. Dari began to cut up some onions to cook a lamb soup in the hearth.

"This is going to take a little while. Go get some fresh air if you want. We haven't been outside all day."

"I think I will. I'll just be down by the lake if you need me."

I took my harp from the case and went out the door. I spoke to the leader of the three guards, an older warrior named Crónan. He nodded and sent the largest of the guards with me. He was the taciturn sort the size of a small mountain with tanned, muscular arms bigger than my thighs. He reminded me of a warrior I had once made love with before I was a nun.

When we reached the lake, I spoke to him: "Would you mind waiting here while I go sit on the beach? I won't be far and you'll be able to see me the whole time."

He grunted and took up his place on a large rock by the water. I walked down the shore about a hundred feet and sat on the sand. The wind was making small waves on the lake and dark clouds were starting to gather in the north. I noticed the first of the leaves on top of the oaks were beginning to turn bright orange and yellow.

I watched the trees and sky for a while, then took out my harp and plucked the strings, making sure it was in tune. A small brown duck swam near and waddled out of the lake in front of me. I composed a song for him:

Autumn, time of harvest, the days are growing short.
  Fields of golden wheat, fruit of the earth.

Deer hiding in the plains with their young,
proud stags hurry from the hills.
Speckled ducks flying south to the sun.
Blackthorn bushes, golden birch, mighty oaks,
trees from ancient times.

"Well, what do you think?" I asked the duck.

"Aaack," it cried, tilting its head to the side.

"It wasn't that bad. I think you're just looking for food. Sorry, my little friend. I left the bread in the hut."

The duck gave me a disdainful look, then waddled back into the water and swam into the shallows to search for fish.

I heard footsteps in the thick woods behind me and saw my guard turn toward the sound with his sword drawn. I couldn't see who was coming, but I saw him bow and put his blade back in its sheath. I stood, knowing who was drawing near.

Áine had two of her own warriors with her. She motioned for them to stay with my man and came down the shore to me. People always say pregnant women glow, but Áine was absolutely radiant in her beauty.

"I'm sorry to intrude on you in this peaceful spot. I know you must have been working all day on the scroll."

"It's no intrusion at all, my lady. It's kind of you to walk all this way to visit me. I would have gladly come to you at the settlement."

"Oh, I needed the exercise. If I don't walk some every day, my legs start to swell. Do you mind if I sit down, though? My back is hurting a bit."

I took off my cloak and spread it on the sand for her, then helped her down. I remembered well from my own pregnancy how hard it could be in the final month. I sat down next to her.

"Thank you. You're very kind."

"It's a pleasure."

"Deirdre, let me begin by saying I'm sorry about yesterday. I behaved rudely, even cruelly, when I found you in the feasting hall. I could plead that being with child has made me irritable, which it certainly has at times, but it wasn't that. You caught me by surprise with your sudden appearance. I know about your past with Cormac. When I saw him holding your hand, some part of me I'm not proud of came bursting out in anger and jealousy."

"Please, Áine, I should be the one apologizing. I showed up at your home unannounced and uninvited. And I admit I took advantage of my old friendship with Cormac to impose on him for refuge. But please let me assure you that whatever Cormac and I once shared is behind us. That was long ago and I'm a nun now. But more than that, Cormac loves you and wouldn't betray his marriage vows to you."

Áine smiled and pulled her cloak more tightly around her. The sun was setting and a cool wind was starting to blow down the steep gap from the mountains at the end of the lake.

"I know. But I also know that Cormac loved you enough just a year ago to ask you to marry him. I was his second choice."

It was hard to deny this. My grandmother once told me that when you're in a hole, don't dig.

"You're right. Cormac did propose to me last year. And yes, I did seriously consider his offer. But I think his proposal was more nostalgia than love."

"I hope you're right," she said. I could tell she wasn't convinced.

"Áine, I watched how Cormac treated you in the hall. His eyes lit up when you walked in the door, even though he was feeling guilty for holding my hand. He looked at you in a way I could only have dreamed of. You're a woman. You can tell as well as I can when a man truly loves you. And Cormac loves you, not me."

She picked up a flat rock from the beach and threw it into the water. It skipped at least five times before it sank into the lake. My duck was still nearby and flew away in alarm.

"I believe you, Deirdre," she said. "But I know the power of old love or nostalgia or whatever you want to call it. I think having you around confuses Cormac. I don't believe he's going to meet you under a tree some night like you did years ago or that he's going to divorce me and marry you. I know he's devoted to me, just as I am to him."

"I'm not trying to confuse him, Áine. I will happily stay here in the hut and not even see him again during this visit. I won't come to the settlement and I promise I'm not going to cause any trouble."

She shook her head. "It's too late for that, Deirdre. You're here and the damage has been done. I'm sure Cormac told you of his plans to expand our kingdom. He dreams of being high king of Ireland someday. If any man could do it, it's him, though I think he's going to have to settle for less in the end. I think it's more likely, with hard work and time, that he could be the most powerful king in Leinster. Glendalough is small, but it's strong in fighting men and has a smart and ambitious young king ruling over it. My father is a good man, but old. His neighboring kingdom on the coast will be Cormac's in a few years if we're patient. Then there's your own tribe under King Dúnlaing, a formidable ruler in spite of his age who nonetheless is even older than my father. His two sons are a bitter disappointment to him and to your whole tribe. I'm betting your people would rather see Cormac rule over them than one of those two. There are other tribes in Leinster who might do the same when they see the prosperity Cormac could bring."

"Yes," I said. "That's all true."

"Deirdre, listen to me. Leinster must have a strong king who can unite our province if we hope to hold back the Uí Néill confederation and the Ulstermen to the north. They've beaten us again and again. If they're not stopped soon, they will rule the whole island."

She put her hand on her belly. "He's kicking. I'm sure it's a boy. Do you want to feel?"

I placed my hand gently on her and felt a sudden kick. For one magical moment I was back on my husband's farm near Kildare, sitting by the hearth and feeling my own son move inside me.

"I don't want my sons to grow up as clients of some Ulster king," she said. "I want them to rule over their own land."

"Yes," I said. "I understand. I think you're right. Cormac would make a fine king to lead us against the Uí Néill. But I don't see how I'm a threat to his ambitions."

"You're smarter than that, Deirdre. You know Cormac can't afford to make any enemies or alienate any potential allies if he wants to expand his kingdom. You Christians are small in numbers, but you have great influence and a network that stretches across the whole island and beyond, all the way to Rome. I admit that I prefer the old ways of the druids and, believe me, we're going to great lengths to stay on good terms with the Order. Cormac is courting the most powerful druids in our land with rich gifts and honors with promises of more if he expands his kingdom. He's even tried to win the favor of your grandmother, a woman he genuinely respects, though she doesn't quite trust him after the heartbreak he caused you."

I remembered in school when Cormac had left me suddenly to return to his father's kingdom. My grandmother was furious and felt that I had been dishonorably seduced and abandoned by a wily prince who should have married me. She threatened to bring him to trial before the druids for the full honor price of his father—enough cattle to ruin his small kingdom—but I talked her out of it with much pleading and many tears.

"You're afraid that helping me will turn the church authorities against Cormac."

"Yes, and you know I'm right. Forgive me, but I was listening outside the armory yesterday when you were talking with Brother Bartholomew. I heard what he said to you. He is going to use the full authority and resources of the church to stop you from translating that scroll. I'm sure he's on the way to Armagh right now to ask the abbot for help, as much as he may dislike him personally. This monk strikes me as a most dangerous enemy, more so because he is not some crazed militant. He's smart and patient and he is going to beat you in the end."

"Maybe, but I've got to try."

"Then try somewhere else. Be practical, Deirdre. Bartholomew knows you're here. We could surround you with a wall of armed warriors, but he will still find a way to get to you and destroy that scroll. You've got to go somewhere far away, and quickly."

She was right. If I stayed at Glendalough, Bartholomew would surely find a way to stop me. And he might move faster than I thought.

"I wish you the best in your work. I hope you tell the world what this Mary of yours had to say. But you can't stay here. If you do, I swear by the gods of my tribe that I will seize that scroll and turn it over to Bartholomew myself."

She rose up slowly and with difficulty, brushing the sand off her legs. She stood facing me and looked every inch the queen she was.

"I won't have you destroying Cormac's chances to be the best king this island has ever known. I won't have you ruining my children's future. You have to leave Glendalough. Now."

"All right, Áine. But won't Cormac be upset that I rejected his hospitality and slipped away in the night?"

She laughed and tossed her hair behind her shoulders. "Of course he will. But you let me worry about Cormac." She leaned in close to me. "Remember, Deirdre, he's *my* husband."

She clapped her hands and her warriors quickly came forward. She spoke a few words to my guard, telling him to inform his captain that Dari and I would be leaving Glendalough that night and that they were to see us safely to the borders of the kingdom. She then turned and walked back into the forest along with her men on the trail to the settlement.

As I watched her go, I envied my friend Cormac to have found such a woman.

Chapter Nine

"And just why are we running away in the middle of the night?"

I had gone back to the hut after Áine left and told Dari we were leaving immediately. I knew she was tired and in no mood to set out in the dark, but I insisted. Crónan and his two men were none too pleased either, but they had their orders from the queen. We all quickly had a bowl of the lamb stew that Dari had made, then packed our things and headed out the door.

"Áine wants us out of Glendalough tonight and I can't say I blame her. If we wait until morning, Cormac would try to stop us. That would lead to a fight between them with us in the middle. I want to be as far away as possible before those two clash."

We took a winding trail above the upper lake over the mountain and south down into the valley of the Little Avon River. Crónan and his men left us on the northern side of the stream since that was the border of Cormac's kingdom. Dari and I waded across the cold waters and headed east downriver toward the coast. But this was only for the sake of Crónan and his men. If anyone asked them where we were going, I wanted them to say they last saw us walking to the sea. Instead, while it was still dark, we turned west through the forest and began the climb over Lugnaquilla, the tallest of the Wicklow Mountains. Dari was not happy.

"Deirdre, I swear by holy Brigid herself, I am going to go back to Kildare if you don't pick a direction and stick to it." She threw down her pack on the rocky ground. We had reached the flat summit of the mountain just as dawn was breaking, and I could see the distant peaks of Britain far across the sea. I pulled a small loaf of bread from my pack and handed half of it to Dari. She took it without a word and began to eat. It was freezing and we both had our blankets wrapped tightly around us.

"Let's find a place to rest for a few hours," I said to her. "Two people walking across the top of this barren mountain are easy to spot from far away. I want to travel by night the next few days until we're far away from Glendalough."

"So where are we going now?"

"I'm not sure yet. Somewhere a great distance from here. Somewhere the church can't reach us. A place where we can finish translating the scroll in peace."

I found some shelter on top of the mountain out of the wind under an overhanging boulder. Chasing an unhappy pine marten from the spot, we climbed down into the rocky den and huddled together in a hole not quite big enough for the two of us.

I put my arm around Dari and hugged her tightly. "I'm sorry about this," I said. "I promise we'll get to a safe place in a few days where we can settle down and finish this job."

"Just make sure it has a warm bed," she mumbled before she fell asleep.

I lay awake trying to think of the kind of place I had promised Dari. Where in Ireland could we hide from the prying eyes of the church among people who would protect us?

It was only a moment before I realized the answer.

I smiled and kissed Dari on the back of her head, then wrapped my blanket around us tightly and was asleep.

For the next two days we walked from sunset to sunrise west across Ireland. There was no time to stop and translate any more of the scroll. I was eager to find out what Mary—or whoever wrote the scroll—had to say. What had happened that changed her life forever? But I was determined to put as much distance between us and Glendalough as possible before we started again.

Two nights later we were in the Slieve Bloom Mountains to the west of Kildare. It was early in the morning and still dark when we finally stopped by an ancient stone tomb near a narrow pass through the mountains. I dared to light a small fire to warm us and cook some trout I had caught a few hours before. This raised Dari's spirits considerably. I only wished we had some spices—aside from the wild garlic I had gathered—to season the fish. The clouds were thick and threatening rain above us. We had walked through the whole night of Samain, the time of Otherworld spirits when no one in their right mind, druid or Christian, would dare to be alone in the wilderness. But we had little choice and in any case there seemed to be no spirits about to bother us in those deserted mountains.

I was hungry. With a quick prayer to all the saints and angels to watch over us, I sprinkled the crushed garlic on the fish with my fingers. Dari was sitting nearby, facing the tomb and fire waiting for the trout to finish cooking.

There was a sudden gust of cold wind that swept through the forest and almost knocked down the trout I had baking over the fire. I grabbed the sticks they were cooking on and held them tightly so they wouldn't fall.

It was then that a dark figure rose above us on top of the tomb. With giant black wings and eyes glowing in the night, it looked like a monstrous raven out of some childhood nightmare.

Dari, who was not easily frightened, screamed and fell backward off the log she was sitting on. I dropped the fish in the fire and reached for the sword in my pack, but was too panicked to find it. We both stared in horror at the monster looming over us.

The figure spoke in a deep and menacing voice: "I am the Morrígan! The goddess of death and despair. Who dares come to my sacred place on this most holy of nights?"

It took me a moment to come to my senses, but finally I lowered my hands from my face and spoke to her.

"Nola, is that you? By the gods, I swear you scared us to death."

"Deirdre?" she asked. "What are you doing down there?"

The figure, who, it was clear now, was just a tall woman wearing a long black cloak, climbed down off the tomb and gave me a warm embrace.

"It's good to see you again," she said. "I don't get many visitors in these mountains."

By now Dari had gotten up from the ground and brushed herself off. She stared at the woman, then at me, in disbelief.

"Deirdre, who on earth is this crazy person? Why is she pretending to be the goddess of death? Does she enjoy scaring people out of their minds in the middle of the night?"

Nola turned to face her with a scowl. "I'm not pretending to be anything, young lady. I *am* the Morrígan. And you would do well to show me some respect."

I put my hand on the visitor's shoulder and took Dari's hand. "Dari," I spoke deliberately, "this is Nola, an honored member of the Order of druids. She is most blessed by the Morrígan, the greatest of the goddesses of our land, who dwells within her when she so chooses."

Dari looked at me for several moments, trying to figure out if I was serious. Then she faced the woman with her palms outstretched before her in supplication. "Nola, honored one, blessed by the goddess, please accept my apology. I was startled and did not realize who you were."

Nola crossed her arms in front of her. She was in her early forties with black hair and the darkest eyes I had ever seen. With her long cloak and pointed hood, she certainly looked like a raven, the sacred bird of the Morrígan, the goddess of battle who bore the honored dead to the Otherworld.

"You are forgiven, my child," she said graciously. "Sometimes I do take people by surprise. But where are my manners? Come with me back to my hut. I have a stuffed chicken cooking in my hearth that will taste much better than those scrawny fish you dropped in the fire. When we're done eating, you can tell me what brings you here."

She went ahead of us down the trail around the tomb. Dari and I collected our things and followed her.

Dari whispered to me as we walked. "Deirdre, she is crazy, isn't she?"

"No, she's not crazy, Dari, just eccentric. But she's perfectly nice if you don't upset her. And if I remember right, she's an excellent cook."

"And her home is where we've been heading to work?"

"No. Honestly, I had forgotten she lived here. But we're far away from everyone in this wilderness, so I think we can rest a day and maybe even translate a little more of the scroll before we move on."

"Move on to where? You must have some destination in mind. Where are we going?"

"Clare Island."

Dari slowly shook her head. "You've got to be kidding," she said.

"I'm not," I replied. "It's the last place anyone from the church would dare to go, especially men."

We caught up to Nola and followed her through the dark forest of pine until we came to a small hut built into the hillside. It was hard to find even if you were looking for it. There were a few chickens scratching the dirt in the yard and a cow wandering in the woods near the stream that ran past the walls of Nola's home.

I was tempted for a moment to stay and finish translating the scroll here if Nola would have us but dismissed the idea since we were still too close to Glendalough and Armagh for my comfort. I wanted a place so distant, so inaccessible, and so unthinkable for a Christian to enter that no one from the church would possibly bother us.

Nola's hut was warm and cozy with two beds, a table with benches, and animal skins scattered about on the floor for warmth. There were also at least a dozen stuffed ravens hanging from the ceiling.

I had met Nola many times at druidic celebrations over the years, but I had only been to her home once years before when I was on my way to sing at a wedding in Connacht. She was what we in the Order call an intermediary. These were a rare and honored group among the druids who had the power of taking the spirit of a god or goddess inside them. Once at a feast I saw a crippled and mute old man who was an intermediary seized by Lug so that he suddenly stood up straight in front of everyone and spoke with a powerful voice proclaiming the will of the god. It was absolutely terrifying to watch. I wasn't quite sure if Nola was truly possessed by the Morrígan or just thought she was, but I wasn't going to do anything to offend her. Besides, the chicken smelled delicious.

"Have a seat, you two. Dinner will be done soon. Or is it breakfast? I don't keep track anymore. Night and day are the same to me. I'm also making a plum pudding. I managed to get some cumin and a small jar of olive oil last time I was at the assembly in Cruachan. I tell you the foreign traders are thieves! If I hadn't threatened to bring down the wrath of the goddess on a British merchant, he would have robbed me blind."

Nola had peeled the plums and cooked them in raisin wine and honey, then mixed them with a dash of cumin along with olive oil and eggs to set it while it cooked. It was baking now on the coals and had a light brown crust on top.

Dari and I went to the well and washed, then came back and helped Nola arrange the food on the table and pour some mead. She offered a brief prayer of thanks to the goddess, then we dug in. It was wonderful. I'm afraid both Dari and I ate more than we should have, which seemed to please Nola. She seldom had guests to appreciate her fine cooking.

When we had finished and Dari and I had cleaned up, Nola asked us what brought us to her forest. I told her about Bartholomew and the scroll. She listened with interest as she drank another cup of mead.

"I remember your Mary," she said. "I was there when the Romans hung her son on that cruel cross. I sat as a raven on his shoulder and watched as his mother wept at his feet. I've seen countless men die in agony on the battlefield, but I have never seen such pain as was in her eyes that day."

Dari looked at me in disbelief. I didn't know what to say, so I changed the subject.

"Nola, we can't stay here long. Bartholomew or his hired men will come after us soon. We're heading to the monastery of the druidic sisters at Clare Island."

"Hmm, I don't know, Deirdre," she said. "They're a strict Order who don't welcome outsiders. You're a druid, but you also wear that cross around your neck. They may not let you in."

"True, but if they will, I can't think of a safer place to finish our work. In the meantime, may we rest here for a day or so? After we sleep for a few hours, I'd like to translate a little more of the scroll, if you would allow it."

"Of course, you can stay and translate all you want. I have to leave for a festival in Cashel, but my home is yours. There's food in the cupboard and you're welcome to all the milk and eggs you want."

"Thank you so much, Nola. We're grateful for your hospitality."

Dari and I said our morning prayers after Nola had left, then crawled into bed. I put the satchel with the scroll under my head and we slept deeply for hours. It was early afternoon before we woke up and had a little more to eat.

"Couldn't we just stay here? This is such a pleasant place, even with all the dead birds. You don't even know if the druid sisters on Clare Island will let us into their monastery. They might end up sacrificing both of us to some bloodthirsty goddess."

"They don't sacrifice anyone, Dari." I sighed. "At least not anymore. That's just a story people tell, though I think the sisters encourage such tales to keep visitors away. But to answer your question, we can't stay here. I know it's nice, but it's too dangerous. Let's translate a little more of the scroll, then pack up and go."

"Are we traveling by night again?" she groaned.

"Yes, at least for a little while longer. It's the safest way to go."

I carried my satchel to the table by the window and took the scroll from the case. Dari sat next to me with her parchment ready to write down what I said. I unrolled the scroll to the point where I had stopped earlier in Glendalough and began.

Chapter Ten

I *'ll never forget that terrible day, Rebekah. It was hot, even for Nazareth, and there was a haze that spread across the horizon all the way to Mount Tabor in the east.*

The Romans came at midday. There were maybe twenty soldiers marching on foot and a centurion on horseback. In the middle of them was a cart pulled by two old horses carrying several Jewish men in heavy chains. The prisoners were filthy and had been badly beaten. One was missing an eye.

Romans never came to Nazareth. I had seen them several times in Sepphoris when I was with Yosef and Yeshua. They were brutish men who said terrible things to women who passed by. If they could get a woman alone, they would do much worse. Most of the time Jews and Greeks alike would hide in their houses and close their shutters when they appeared. But the sight of Roman soldiers in our village was so odd that the people of the town began to gather in the square where the cart had stopped.

The centurion got off his horse and handed the reins to one of his men. He ordered his soldiers to take the prisoners out of the cart. The men were forced out at spearpoint and stumbled across the square to collapse next to the well. Half the soldiers stood guard near them while the other half took their places next to the centurion who stood facing us.

He scowled and spoke to us in our own language:

"Listen to me, you Jewish scum. We don't want to be in this shithole of a town any more than you want us here, but the axle on our cart is broken and needs repair. These rebels are on their way to Caesarea to be crucified. If it were up to me I'd kill the whole damn lot of you, but for now I'll settle for these bastards. And don't

get any ideas about helping them escape. If any of you go near them or even look at them, I swear by Jupiter's balls I will cut your throats. Do we understand each other?"

The villagers all backed away. Mothers pulled their children close.

"Now, which one of you is the carpenter?"

I started to reach out and hold Yosef back, but I knew as well as he did that things would be worse if he tried to hide himself. It was best for him to fix the cart quickly so the Romans would go. There was nothing we could do for the poor men they were taking to their deaths.

Yosef went to the centurion and the man told him to get his tools. Four of the soldiers lifted the back of the empty cart onto some stone blocks so that Yosef could crawl underneath. As a carpenter's wife, I knew at a glance the axle was cracked and needed replacing. Yosef sent Yeshua, who had just turned eighteen, to his workshop to bring his tools and one of the oak timbers he stored in the rafters. Then he and my son began their work.

It took a couple of hours to remove the old axle, shape the new one to size, and refit the wheels onto it. I watched and worried from the front of our house. I saw everyone else in town doing the same from their own homes. The

Jewish prisoners sat in the hot sun by the well the whole time, but the Romans gave them nothing to drink.

When Yosef and Yeshua had finished, the centurion inspected the work and seemed satisfied. He offered no payment, nor did Yosef expect any.

While Yosef and the centurion were still near the cart, Yeshua walked to the well with a bucket. The bored soldiers guarding the prisoners let him pass, thinking he was getting water for himself after the hot work. But when he had filled the bucket, my son took the common cup hanging by the well and went to where the prisoners were sitting. He dipped the cup into the bucket of cool water and offered it to the nearest man.

Everything happened so fast then. The centurion saw what Yeshua was doing and shouted to his men to stop him. The startled soldiers knocked the cup from Yeshua's hand and pushed him roughly to the ground so that he hit his head hard against the stones. The centurion ran to the well and raised his sword above my son. But before he could bring down the blade, Yosef threw himself on the man from behind with all his might and knocked him into the dirt. The soldiers grabbed Yosef and held him up by the arms while the furious centurion got to his feet. The people of *the town had all rushed out of their houses. I ran forward to my son and husband.*

There was a moment frozen in time when my eyes met Yosef's. We both knew what was going to happen next, but we also knew there was nothing we could do to stop it. In that brief moment we said farewell.

The centurion plunged his sword into Yosef's belly and angled it upward to pierce his heart. The Romans let him fall to the ground in a pool of his own blood.

The centurion turned then to Yeshua. My son was lying on the ground unconscious or even dead for all I knew. I did the only thing I could think of and covered his body with my own. I could feel his heart still beating beneath me. I wept and kissed him and waited for the blow that would kill us both.

But the centurion stopped. Whether the death of Yosef had been enough to satisfy his rage or because he thought Yeshua was already as good as dead, he put his sword back in its sheath and walked away.

He called to his soldiers to get the prisoners back into the cart. I lay clinging to Yeshua as they loaded the men and left Nazareth.

The women of the town at last came forward to help. They took Yeshua from me and carried him to his bed in our house. I knelt by my Yosef, whose soul had gone to be with the Almighty. I remember thinking that this was the very spot where he had saved me from being stoned to death years before. I kissed him and covered his body with my cloak. I knew then that nothing would ever be the same again.

Chapter Eleven

C lare Island is only a short distance off the western coast of Ireland, but it seems far away when you stand on the rocky shore of Clew Bay gazing out into the Atlantic. The island itself is fairly small, with a low black mountain looming over its western end. Far to the south of the bay are the distant hills of Connemara, while to the east is an ancient peak sacred to the goddess of the sun, though in recent years Christians had built a shrine to Patrick on its summit and begun making pilgrimages there. Some must have prayed to God and Patrick alike for protection against the forces of darkness as they stood on the mountain and stared across the waters at the forbidden island.

Dari and I had arrived at the shore after a four-night march west across Ireland from Nola's hut which included a harrowing midnight crossing at a ford on the flooded Shannon River. We had spent the last day sleeping fitfully in a dense grove of trees near the coast. Even then I wouldn't let Dari light a small fire. It was probably my imagination, but I couldn't shake the feeling that danger was close behind us.

"So how are we going to get there?" asked Dari. "If you plan to swim, I'm staying here."

"No, we're not going to swim. The water is freezing and it's too far anyway. Besides, I've got to protect the scroll. We need to find someone to take us."

"Who would dare to row us across? I've heard scary stories about this place my whole life."

"People do sometimes visit, Dari. The sisters there aren't total recluses. It's just that they strongly discourage anyone they haven't invited. And of course, no men are ever allowed to set foot there."

"What about nuns?" she asked.

"That remains to be seen."

We began walking along the shore. Soon we came across a skinny girl sitting on a curragh mending her fishing nets. She was no more than thirteen, with curly red hair.

"Greetings, daughter," I said.

"Hello," she answered warily.

"My name is Sister Deirdre and this is Sister Dari. We are holy women of the monastery of Brigid in Kildare come to visit the sisters on Clare Island. We're looking for someone who will take us across."

"Well, good luck with that," she said, turning her head away. "The ladies there don't welcome outsiders and I'm sure not going to risk my life. I heard they sacrifice trespassers to the gods."

"Young lady," I said, drawing myself up tall and taking my harp from its case. "I am a bard and a member of the Order of the druids. The sisters of Clare Island will welcome me. I promise you will return home safely with a handsome reward if you row us across."

She was still hesitant. "I don't know. I don't think my ma would let me if she were here."

"I think your mother would be most pleased that you helped a high-ranking bard. I doubt she would like the satire I could compose against your family if you refuse me."

That did it. I felt terrible about scaring her like that and normally wouldn't have done such a thing, but I was desperate to get to the island. The poor girl was frightened with good reason. In a land where honor was valued above all, a bard could destroy a family's reputation for generations by composing a satire against them.

The girl flipped the boat over and quickly dragged it down to the shore. It was surprisingly light and was small and round, like most curraghs, with tanned cattle skins stretched over a frame of sturdy birch wood. I put my harp back into its case and climbed into the boat along with Dari, careful to step only onto the frame. The girl pushed us out into the water and took her place kneeling in the middle of the boat with two short oars. I had worried that she might be too frail to handle the curragh, but she was clearly experienced at hauling heavy loads of fish. She was fast in the water and didn't even make a splash as she dug deeply into the waves.

It wasn't long before the island was drawing close. I couldn't see anyone on the shore, which worried me. We were clearly visible as we crossed the bay. I had expected someone to be waiting for us.

"Ma'am," the girl said, "would it be all right if I didn't pull all the way up on the shore? My ma said I would be cursed forever if I even touched the rocks on the beach."

"Yes, just pull up into the shallows and we'll wade in from there."

I climbed out of the boat when we were near shore and held it steady while Dari crawled out into water up to our knees. I reached into my case and pulled out a golden pendant on a thin silver chain that had been given to me by a king years ago in payment for a song of praise at a festival. I had at least a dozen like it, but the girl's mouth dropped at what for her must have been an unimaginable treasure.

"Take it," I said, "and may the blessing of a bard be upon you and your family."

The girl took it, then bowed her head to me and set out again across the bay. She was far from shore by the time Dari and I reached land.

"Well, we're here now," Dari said. "I was expecting a guard of Amazon warriors with flaming swords or some such thing from the stories I've heard about this place."

"The sisters aren't violent, Dari, just very private. I've never been here, but I know they're an ancient Order of druidic women who practice prayer and devotion to the goddesses protecting our island. Some people say they kept the Romans from invading us years ago by stirring up frequent storms in the eastern sea."

"Do you believe that?"

"I don't honestly know. I'm a Christian, but I believe the gods are real. I don't want to dismiss them or their power."

We walked along the beach until we came to a trail through the heather leading inland. There were low rock walls on either side with sheep grazing behind them, but no sign of people.

"Deirdre, this is unnerving. Shouldn't we stop and wait for them to come to us? I feel like a trespasser watched by a thousand eyes."

"I feel it too, but I want to keep going. I know their monastery is at the base of the mountain. Let's approach them openly and hope for the best."

Storm clouds had gathered thickly now and a cold rain was starting to fall. Soon it was coming down in buckets. I was worried about the scroll and held the case tightly to my chest to shield it from the water. Then suddenly we were at the end of the trail beneath a high wall of unworked stones with a massive wooden gate. On the gate was a large iron knocker in the shape of three intertwining circles.

"So what do we do now, Deirdre?" Dari was soaked to the skin and the rain was running down her face like a waterfall. She now looked more miserable than frightened.

I reached up to the knocker. But before I could touch it, the gate began to swing slowly open. We looked at each other, then I took a deep breath and entered first.

Inside the gate was a beautiful garden with autumn flowers that had been carefully cultivated. In the center of the garden was the largest apple tree I had ever seen. It must have been at least a century old, with dozens of bright red apples hanging from its branches. Inside the walls of the garden, there was no rain at all, whether by coincidence or magic I couldn't say.

The gate closed behind us and I turned to see a small elderly woman in a white cloak and hood sliding a large iron bolt back into place.

Dari and I both bowed to her.

"Sister, my name is Deirdre. I am a member of the Order of druids and a bard who . . ."

The woman put her finger to her mouth and shook her head. I had never heard that the sisters of Clare Island followed a vow of silence, but I wasn't going to offend them. I stopped speaking and nodded. The woman led us through the garden along a smooth stone path toward what must have been the main house of the monastery. Most of the other structures scattered throughout the garden were typical thatched huts, but this building, like the outside walls, was made of large stones closely fitted without mortar and roofed with thick oak timbers overlaid with wooden shingles.

Our silent guide ushered us through a side door into a windowless room with a single bench on one side. Hanging from the wall on hooks were tunics and two white robes, along with thick wool socks and sandals. She motioned for us to remove our wet clothing, which she took out of the room, locking the door from the outside.

Dari and I stood naked and shivering on the stone floor.

"Well," Dari said, "what do we do now?"

"They must mean for us to wear these robes," I said. "Why else would we be here?"

"You mean locked naked in a stone cell? I don't know, maybe this is what they do to trespassers before they sacrifice them on a bloody altar."

"Dari, don't worry. We'll be fine."

At least I hoped so.

We must have waited in that dark room for an hour before the same silent woman returned and led us down the empty hallway to a large room with a long table and two tall windows of glass, a rare luxury. Behind the table was a silver-haired woman, apparently the abbess, about fifty years of age in the same white robes we now wore. Around her neck she wore the simple golden torque of a druid. She nodded to our guide, who withdrew and closed the door.

"Well, well. Sisters Deirdre and Dari, Christian nuns of the monastery of holy Brigid at Kildare. You come on an urgent task pursued by powerful enemies. And you have in your case an ancient scroll that may preserve the words of Mary, the mother of your god."

Dari and I stood speechless.

"Reverend Mother, how could you possibly know that?" I asked.

"Like your grandmother, Deirdre, I am a seer. And when I look at you, I see trouble."

She motioned for us to sit on the bench by the table and brought bread and cheese from a large dish in the corner. She also poured us two large cups of wine.

"Eat and drink," she said. "You must be starving after your journey. I'll wait till you're done to tell you about all the problems you're going to cause us."

We were indeed very hungry and ate everything on the plate. The wine was superb. I had never tasted anything like it.

"We make it from our own apples," the abbess said, taking a long drink from her own cup, "though we blend it with a grape vintage we have shipped from Gaul, a reminder of a time long ago."

When I had finished eating, I put the plate aside and addressed the abbess. "Reverend Mother . . ."

"Deirdre," she said, "you don't need to give me such an exalted title. On this island we call each other by family names. The others you will meet should be addressed simply as 'sister.' As the leader of our monastery, those under my direction call me 'Mother.' You may also call me that if you wish."

"Of course, Mother. May I ask what you know of us and what of our task I should explain?"

"I know," she said, "only what I have already told you. As I'm sure your grandmother has told you, the vocation of a seer is an inexact science. We know only what is revealed to us by the gods. Emotions, patterns, scattered images and words. It's not like reading a book."

"But you knew what we carried and who was after us," said Dari.

"Yes, that I could see, but little more. I confess I knew your names long before today. You have quite a reputation in Ireland, Deirdre—as a bard, of course, but also as someone with great courage and more than her share of recklessness. And I knew your friend Dari must be with you since your names are often spoken in the same breath. A bond of friendship so close is a gift of the gods. I envy you."

"But Mother," I said, "you implied that we would be trouble to you here. We have no wish to be. We will leave now if you would like us to."

"No, Deirdre." She shook her head. "I want you to stay. One thing I do sense is that the work you have been given is of great importance. I don't know if the words in your scroll are those of Mary or not, but I sense that some higher power wants you to finish your task. Whether this power is your Christian god I cannot say. But we will help you however we can by providing you refuge and protection. We don't have much here, but what we have is yours."

"Thank you, Mother," Dari and I said at the same time.

"You two even speak together!" She smiled. "But when I said trouble was coming, I meant it. I sense that the forces working against you are gathering their resources to seek you out. They will find you here, sooner or later, that I can see. You must work quickly."

"We will, Mother," I said.

"We will provide you with quarters for living and working. You may join us for our daily meals or I will have food sent to your room. Feel free to roam the grounds and garden as you wish. We have no secrets here. You are also welcome to join us for worship if you would like. I think you would find it not so different from your own Christian services."

"You are most kind, Mother," I said.

Dari spoke up. "Mother, please forgive my curiosity, but I've heard stories about your monastery all my life. Some of them quite fantastic. Are you really able to work magic? Can you control the wind and waves? Do you really perform human sacrifice?"

"Dari!" I said out of the side of my mouth.

The abbess laughed gently. "My child, don't believe everything you hear. We do encourage some stories to keep the curious away, but we don't even offer animals to the gods here. The sheep you saw are for wool and milk only. We also have chickens for eggs, but we don't eat meat of any kind. Outside of worship, we practice silence for the sake of contemplation as much as possible, but talking is not forbidden. We are an order devoted to prayer and contemplation, seeking only to bring balance to an unbalanced world."

"Then how did the stories of human sacrifice arise?" Dari asked.

"Long ago, our monastery was located on an island at the mouth of the Loire River in southern Gaul.

When Caesar and his legions invaded that land almost six hundred years ago, we knew we were no longer safe there. We came here to this distant island far from Rome. While we were still in Gaul, we did on rare occasions offer up one of our members to the gods in sacrifice, but those women were always volunteers of particular devotion. We haven't done such a thing for centuries, but such stories do not easily die."

"We've bothered you enough, Mother," I said. "I can't speak for Dari, but I would be honored to attend one of your services. However, we still have several hours of light remaining today, so for now perhaps you could have one of the sisters show us to our room so we could continue our work on the scroll. I too feel that we are racing against time."

"Of course," the abbess said, then clapped her hands.

Our silent guide returned. We bowed deeply to the abbess and followed the sister to a bright and pleasant room on the far side of the building. I could hear the voices of women chanting somewhere in the distance.

"They seem very nice," Dari said. "I'm sorry I asked about the magic and sacrifices, but I didn't know if I would have another chance."

"It's fine, Dari. The abbess wasn't offended."

There were two comfortable chairs and a wide desk in our room below a set of large glass windows facing south. There was also a box of tallow candles in the corner and a jar of apple wine on a table next to a large bed covered in thick fleeces. It looked so cozy that I wanted to lie down and sleep for the rest of the day, but I knew we were running out of time. Bartholomew's men were coming.

Chapter Twelve

*I*t was three days before Yeshua woke up and weeks before he could walk again. I fed him rich broth while he lay in bed, but he had lost so much weight that he looked more like a corpse than a man. It was several months before he was strong enough to work again in the carpenter's shop.

You can imagine what it was like for me then, Rebekah. You lost your own husband to the Romans not so long ago.

I was a widow now in a world that was not kind to widows. The women of the town brought me a little food while Yeshua was still in bed, but the harvest had been poor that year and everyone was hungry. When he was better, Yeshua took small jobs around town in exchange for some barley flour or sometimes a little olive oil. Often he would have to walk all the way to Sepphoris to find work for the day. In the evenings he would teach the boys of the village in exchange for an occasional chicken, but I knew he would have taught them for nothing. It was the only time I saw joy in his eyes those months after Yosef died.

On Shabbat, Yeshua would lead the men of Nazareth in prayer and recite the Torah in a clear voice that carried well beyond our little synagogue. People passing through Nazareth would often stop just to listen to him. His sermons were more stories than admonitions. Most rabbis would chastise their people and demand stricter obedience to the law. Yeshua instead told simple tales of everyday life as examples of how we could all draw closer to the Almighty. Even the most hardened old men in town would listen to him in wonder.

In the years that followed we struggled to survive, but then so did everyone else in Galilee. The harvests continued to be poor, not that it mattered to the tax collectors. They would come into Nazareth every year with their guards, men too brutish and drunken to find work as soldiers among the Romans. They would go house to house and take whatever they wanted. Yeshua tolerated them better than most. He told me once they were victims of the Romans as much as we were. He even struck up a friendship with one tax collector named Mattityahu who would come and stand in the back of the synagogue and listen to my Yeshua preach.

It was during this time that a young couple who were our neighbors brought their daughter Tabitha to Yeshua. She was perhaps three years old and had suffered from violent convulsions since she was a baby. The old women of the village said she was possessed by a demon and urged her parents to leave her on the far side of the mountain to die. But the couple loved their little girl and did their best to care for her. It was after the service one Shabbat when Yeshua was moving his carpentry tables back into place that they carried Tabitha to him and asked him to pray for her. Her convulsions had gotten worse lately and they were afraid she would die soon.

Yeshua sat down on a bench in the corner of the workshop and held Tabitha in his lap. It made me happy and sad to see him with children. He was so good with them, but he had not *talked of finding a wife since Yosef died. I would mention it to him from time to time, as a mother does, but he would laugh and say one woman in his life was more than he could handle.*

We were alone that morning with Tabitha and her parents. As the girl sat on his lap, Yeshua began to sing to her a song that I had never heard. It was a beautiful tune with words I couldn't understand, words of light and joy more of heaven than of earth. Tabitha was smiling at him with her bright eyes the whole time while her parents stared at Yeshua, not knowing what to think.

Tabitha's convulsions had become so frequent that she could barely eat or sleep. Her legs had never been strong enough for her to walk, so her father or mother carried her everywhere. Yet when Yeshua had finished his song, he sat her gently on the ground and told her to go to her parents. Her mother started to come forward to pick her up, but Yeshua held up his hand to stop her. Then before our eyes, Tabitha started to get up using her arms to steady herself. She fell down once, but then tried again and at last stood on her own thin legs. The child laughed and stretched out her arms to her parents, and then—let the Almighty be my witness—she ran across the room to her mother.

The parents gasped in astonishment and hugged their little girl tightly as they wept. They knelt before Yeshua thanking him, but he lifted them up and told them to give thanks to the Almighty, who was the source of all healing. He then asked them not to tell anyone what had happened.

When they had gone, I went to Yeshua and stood before him. He was still a little boy in my eyes, but he had grown into a man a foot taller than me. I looked up at him and he smiled.

I had always known who he was, ever since the messenger of the Almighty had come to me years before. But then again, I had never really known.

"Yeshua, how did you do that?"

"I did nothing, Mother. It's the Almighty who heals the body and soul."

"But that song, where did you learn it? It was so beautiful."

He shrugged as boys will do. "It just came to me."

"Yeshua, people will hear of this. They will tell others. How could they not?"

"Then people will hear, Mother. I've got to finish putting the furniture back in place."

He kissed me on the cheek and started moving the tables again.

Of course everyone heard. Within the week people were coming from as far away as Magdala to be healed. They brought sick children and elderly parents. One man even brought a lame donkey for Yeshua to bless. Some offered my son gold and silver coins to heal the ones they loved, but he would take nothing. He prayed with each of them and sent them on their way.

When winter came there were fewer visitors. Everyone was too busy with the harvest, which for the first time in years was abundant. After a long day in the fields, Yeshua came home to dinner. I could tell he had something on his mind. He had been quiet for days and lost in his own thoughts.

"Mother," he said as I put away the dishes, "there's something I need to tell you."

"And what is that, my son?"

"I'm going away."

"Away to where? Sepphoris? Is there work there? When will you be back?"

"No, not Sepphoris. And I don't know that I'll ever be back."

Suddenly I could barely breathe. My heart was pounding in my chest. I sat down on a stool near the hearth. Somehow I had always known this day would come.

Yeshua sat down next to me and put his arm around my shoulder. "There's something I need to do, Mother, and I can't do it in Nazareth. I want to learn, to study with the wisest rabbis of the land, to become something more than I can be here."

"But you are already a wise rabbi, Yeshua, and a great healer."

"There are enough healers wandering this land, Mother. Some have a true gift from the Almighty, but most are thieves stealing money from those who have lost hope. Healing isn't what I want to do with my life. I want to be a teacher. Our people have lost hope, especially the poor. They think the Almighty has forgotten them, that he has left them to perish under the heel of the Romans. But it isn't the Romans who are our enemies. There will always be oppressors in this world. It was the Egyptians or Babylonians or Persians for our ancestors. For us it's the Romans, but there will be others until the end of the age. We think that if we could only throw off the yoke of the Romans, we could rule ourselves and all would be well. But the kingdom of the Almighty isn't on this earth. It dwells inside each of us if only we will do his will."

"Yeshua," I said, "you must follow where the Almighty leads you. I won't stand in your way. I'll be fine here. Or maybe I'll go live with my sister in Ramah. Her daughter just had twins and could use help with the babies."

Yeshua smiled at me. "I'm not leaving you behind. How could I live without my mother to take care of me?"

"But where would we go?"

"Kefar Nahum—or Capernaum as the Romans call it. Remember, I was there last year for a couple of weeks working on the new docks? I made some friends among the fishermen, especially a burly fellow named Shimon. They call him Kephas, the Rock—either for his steadfastness or his thick head, I'm not sure which. I know we could stay with him and his family for a while. You'd like his mother-in-law. She comes from Endor, just over the mountain from here."

"I know where Endor is, Yeshua. But why go to live in Kefar Nahum among fishermen if you want to study the law?"

"Because there's a school there run by the disciples of Rabbi Hillel, the leader of the Sanhedrin who died recently. When I was in Kefar Nahum, I would study with them in the evenings. I even heard Hillel's grandson Gamaliel speak one Shabbat when he passed through the town. The Pharisees at the school are learned men who care about the poor of our land, more *so than the followers of Rabbi Shammai, though he too is a great scholar."*

"How will you make a living?"

"As I always have, as a carpenter. The town is booming and there are plenty of jobs. Most of the students there work during the day and study at the school in the evenings and on Shabbat."

"I don't know, Yeshua. I've lived here most of my life. You know how the people around the lake talk about our town. They think they're better than us. 'Can anything good come from Nazareth?' is one of their favorite jokes."

"Mother, they're not that bad. You can show them how—what's the Greek word?—sophisticated a woman of Nazareth can be."

"You're mocking me now, Yeshua," I said as I pushed him away, though I couldn't help but laugh.

"It will be an adventure. You'll see."

"I'm too old for adventures, Yeshua, but I suppose I'll go with you."

"Thank you," he said as he kissed me. "I'd be lost without you, you know."

"You certainly would, Yeshua. And don't you forget that."

"I won't, Mother. And don't worry. I'll never leave you."

Chapter Thirteen

The evening meal at the monastery that night was a thick porridge of creamed vegetables with freshly baked bread and honey butter. There were also several jugs of excellent beer. The porridge had a hint of coriander in it, an herb of southern Europe that I had tasted only once before when I visited a rich king in Munster. How the sisters on this remote island had gotten it I couldn't say, but I was beginning to realize they were full of surprises.

The meal was eaten in silence aside from a few hushed whispers between the sisters. I took the opportunity to study them as we all sat on our benches around the long wooden table. There were about thirty of them ranging in age from a few novices in their teens to one ancient woman who looked like she had escaped from Gaul when Caesar invaded. The abbess sat at the head of the table. I had somehow expected them to be solemn in their silence, but they were just the opposite. I had never seen a group of people who seemed so content and even joyful. The sisters and brothers at our monastery in Kildare were all good people—well, most of them—but we had our bad days and petty quarrels. I couldn't imagine these women ever arguing with one another. I'm sure they had their moments, but their sense of peace practically filled the room.

At the start of the meal the abbess introduced Dari and me to the sisters, but I had the feeling they already knew all about us. She also let us know that their evening worship would convene an hour after supper in the hall of prayer just next door. Since it was too dark to work on the scroll anymore that day, Dari and I walked to the garden when the blessing of dismissal had been recited.

"Do you want to go to the worship service, Dari?" I asked.

"Normally I would, but I feel like I'm walking in my sleep. Do you think they would be offended if I missed tonight? I'd be happy to go tomorrow."

"I don't think they would be offended at all. In fact I'm having trouble imagining what would perturb these ladies."

"I know what you mean. I thought we had something special at Kildare. I'm very happy there and I think most of the other sisters and brothers are too, but there's something, I don't know, magical about this place. I feel like I've crossed over into the Otherworld."

"Maybe we have. In the old stories, the Otherworld is often found on islands in the western sea. But it isn't always a place as much as it is a state of being, like an idea that lives inside us."

"That sounds like how Jesus describes the kingdom of God, both in the Gospels and in our scroll." She hesitated. "Deirdre, have you made up your mind yet about whether or not those are Mary's words?"

"No, I'm not certain yet. But try as I might—and I have tried—I can't find anything false about it. Everything in the scroll fits well with what we know from the Bible. And the voice telling the story sounds real. But I'm still not sure."

Dari and I were walking slowly around the apple tree as we talked. I wanted to reach up and take a piece of fruit, but I wasn't sure it was allowed. This place was too much like Eden already for me to start playing Eve.

A sister about our age had been watching us as we walked in the garden. I could tell she wanted to approach us but was hesitant to disturb our peace. But no sooner had I thought about eating an apple than she came over to us and picked two of the largest and ripest ones and handed them to Dari and me.

"You looked like you might want one of these," she said to us both with a smile.

"Thank you, sister," I said. "I wasn't sure if it was permitted."

"There is very little forbidden here, Deirdre. We try to follow the ways of nature and listen to the voices of the divine speaking to our hearts."

I nodded, but Dari looked like she wasn't convinced.

"Forgive me, sister . . . ," she started to say.

"You can call me Olwen if you want, Dari. We aren't so formal with outsiders."

"Olwen is a British name," I said.

"Yes, I came here about ten years ago from a farm near the wall the Roman emperor Hadrian built. Several of the sisters are British. One is even from Brigantium in Spain, where they maintain the old ways in spite of centuries of Roman rule."

"Thank you, Olwen," Dari said. "I always feel more comfortable using a person's real name. I didn't mean to look doubtful when you spoke about the ways of nature and listening to our hearts, but that seems, forgive me, a bit vague as a guide to life."

Olwen laughed softly. "I sometimes think so too, especially when the gods seem to be telling each of the sisters different things. But the abbess says that if we're at peace and listen carefully to the still, small voice of the divine in our hearts, then we'll know what to do."

"That sounds like a passage from our Bible," I said. "We read it in our own services."

Olwen closed her eyes and began to speak:

> And, behold, the Lord passed by, and a great and mighty wind tore through the mountains, and broke in pieces the rocks before the Lord; but the Lord was not in the wind. And after the wind an earthquake; but the Lord was not in the earthquake. And after the earthquake a fire; but the Lord was not in the fire. And after the fire a still, small voice.

"That's what your prophet Elijah discovers in the first book of Kings in the Jewish scriptures," Olwen said. "I hope I'm remembering it right."

"How do you know about Elijah, Olwen?" I asked. "Were you raised as a Christian?"

"No one in my hometown in Britain was a Christian. We all followed the old ways. I studied to be a druid from the time I was a little girl. I learned the stories of the Bible here on this island. It's an important part of our training to learn and appreciate holy works from many lands."

"But doesn't that cause conflicts with what you believe as a druid?" Dari asked.

"You might ask Deirdre that," Olwen said. "I think she tries to live in two worlds at the same time."

I wondered how she knew that. "It isn't always easy," I said. "Being both a Christian and a druid can get complicated."

"It isn't supposed to be easy," Olwen answered gently. "We find harmony with many of our own beliefs in the teachings of other religions, but we find challenges too. We were just listening to the creation stories of the Greeks recently during our study time. Their poet Hesiod sings of such violence among their gods in the beginning of the world. But as one of our sisters observed, each human life comes into this world through blood and pain, so perhaps the Greeks have a point."

"You have books here?" I asked.

"Oh yes, quite a few. We all know Latin, so we use translations into that language, but some of the sisters are quite good scholars of other tongues, including those of the Persians and ancient Egyptians. We even have a few translations of texts from India and Cathay that we've collected by way of merchants in Constantinople and Alexandria."

"You should meet Father Ailbe, from our monastery," I said. "He's from Alexandria and has traveled in India. He would be fascinated to talk with you all."

"I wish we could meet him," Olwen said. "But unfortunately men aren't allowed on our island."

"Why is that?" asked Dari. "Is it to keep you pure from the ways of the world?"

Olwen laughed again. This time several of the sisters in the garden looked at us with surprise and a touch of disapproval. Olwen looked contrite.

"Sorry about that," she said. "The sisters already think I'm a little too animated. Must be my British heritage. We like to laugh where I come from."

"We don't want to get you into trouble," Dari said.

"Oh, I'm not in trouble. Like I said, we don't have many rules. It's just that you seem to think we're like the vestal virgins of ancient Rome."

"You mean you're not . . . celibate?" I asked delicately.

"No." She smiled. "A least, most of us aren't. We're allowed to leave the island whenever we want to seek out male company—or female, if we prefer. Intimate relations between the sisters here in our small monastery would make life too complicated. We usually stay on the island, but a few times a year most of us will journey to the mainland for a romantic rendezvous. As long as we're discreet about it, the abbess doesn't object."

"But what about the risk of pregnancy?" Dari asked.

"Oh, we've mastered the art of not getting pregnant when we don't want to. But children are not unknown here. If a sister wants to have a child, she's welcome to do so. Again, we see children as part of the pattern of nature. The girls born here will often stay and become sisters themselves. The boys must leave when they reach puberty, but their mothers are welcome to visit them on the mainland whenever they want. We have one sister on the island pregnant now and two young children with us. You may see them before you leave. They are remarkably well behaved since they're raised in such quiet, peaceful surroundings."

"We have plenty of children at our monastery," Dari said. "But they're students at our school."

Olwen put her hand on Dari's and looked at her kindly. "You wish you could have a child, don't you?"

Dari took in a short breath, then spoke softly. "How did you know I couldn't?"

"I sensed it, more from the way you spoke than by any magic, as you call it. One advantage to being silent most of the time is that you learn how to read people pretty well."

"You're right," Dari said. "I can't have children. I always wanted to. Even when I was married to a horrible man, I still prayed to the gods that they would stir a life within me. But it wasn't possible. I take joy though in the children that I teach. They're like my own."

"Dari," Olwen said gently, "it may be possible for you to bear a child. I can't promise you anything, but we have ancient ways here that can make it possible for most women to become pregnant, even if they haven't been able to before."

"I could have a child?" Dari asked.

"Probably," Olwen said. "Again, I can't say for sure, but I wouldn't bring it up if I wasn't fairly certain."

"I . . . I don't know," Dari said as she looked at me. "It would mean renouncing my vows and leaving the monastery. Kildare is my life. The work with the children, the worship, the service to others. How could I put all that behind me?"

"Dari," I said, "you don't have to decide anything now. I need your help to finish the translation of the scroll anyway."

"She's right," Olwen said. "Just know that we're always here if you decide it's what you want to do."

"Thank you, Olwen. It would be a great gift."

A bell rang softly in the hall of prayer announcing the gathering for evening worship.

"Olwen," Dari said, "I'm very tired and you've given me a lot to think about. Would you mind if I go to bed instead of coming to the service?"

"Not at all. I know you're exhausted after your journey." Olwen kissed her on the cheek. "Sleep in peace, Dari. There is nothing here to fear."

Dari left us and walked back into the main building.

"You should probably rest too, Deirdre."

"I will soon enough," I said, "but I'd like to attend your service. I've worshipped with both Christians and druids, but never at a place like this. I'm curious. I also wouldn't mind a little divine inspiration."

"Then please join us."

We left the garden and followed the line of other sisters making their way into the hall of worship.

I don't know what I had been expecting. Most druidic temples were outdoors and stark in their simplicity. They were usually roofless enclosures surrounded by plain wood or unworked stone, always with an altar for animal sacrifice in front. But more often than not, druids would gather in dark oak groves and chant hymns to the gods.

The hall of worship at Clare Island was something else entirely. From the moment I entered through the massive wooden doors, I was almost blinded by light and color. The brightly painted walls were hung with gorgeous tapestries of vast, swirling geometric images and stylized forms of every kind of animal—birds, seals, wolves, along with a few elephants and dragons. Even the ceiling was covered with colored panels of the goddesses of our land and the pageantry of creation. The effect was all the more remarkable because of the careful placement of polished bronze panels throughout the hall to catch and reflect the light of hundreds of candles.

"Jesus, Mary, and Joseph!" I heard myself say without thinking. Suddenly I was afraid I might have violated one of the few rules of the monastery by speaking inside the sacred hall.

An older woman behind me whispered in my ear. "Don't worry, Deirdre. I'm sure your holy family would be impressed too. It really is something, isn't it?"

I nodded and vowed to myself to stay silent for the rest of the service.

⚇

"What was it like?" Dari asked me later that night when I had returned to our room and crawled into bed.

"I'm not sure I can describe it very well," I answered. "There were no spoken words or prayers as such, only songs. A few I recognized, but most of them were new and strange to me. Some songs didn't even use words, just harmonies of sound, with the sisters singing different parts. The effect was astonishing, unlike anything I've ever experienced in a druid or Christian ceremony. I know it sounds silly, but it was as if my soul was filled with light."

"I can't wait to go to the service tomorrow evening," she said. "I could use a little light in my soul."

"Did Olwen upset you with the talk about having a child?" I asked.

"No, not at all. She just caught me off guard. Do you really think it's possible?"

"I don't know," I answered. "But I would never underestimate these women. I think it's quite likely they have ancient knowledge that most druids have forgotten. I've heard stories from the old days of women bearing children through the intercession of supernatural powers. We call it magic, but I think the sisters here would see it as being in harmony with the patterns of nature and listening to the goddesses who give life to the world."

"But if I wanted to become pregnant," she said, "I would have to leave the monastery at Kildare. I'd also have to find a man who would want to marry me."

"I don't think that would be a problem, Dari. You're still young."

"I'm thirty years old. Most women marry in their teens."

"Thirty is young enough. There are plenty of men who would welcome a wife as kind and beautiful as you. What about Senchán?"

"What about him?"

"He's a good man and a hard worker with a farm near the monastery. His wife died last year and I know he likes you. I've seen the way he looks at you when he brings his little girl to school."

"Senchán? Really?"

"Don't tell me you haven't noticed."

"I'm a nun, Deirdre. I'm not supposed to notice such things. I do like Senchán though. He's a loving father who was always kind to his wife. But forgetting about men for a moment, the real question is do I want to give up my life at the monastery? I'm not sure I do, even to have a child." She squeezed my hand. "And I would hate to leave you," she added.

"Well, you don't have decide anything now. Let's finish translating the scroll and get back to Kildare, then we can sort out everything. Maybe you could cook some of your seasoned mussels for Senchán? They say food is the way to a man's heart. As for his other parts, you'll have to use your imagination."

"You're terrible, Deirdre. Go to sleep."

"Good idea. I want to get an early start translating tomorrow."

Chapter Fourteen

A nd so, Rebekah, Yeshua and I moved to Kefar Nahum that summer. It was hectic there after my quiet life in Nazareth. There were local Jewish fishermen, Greek merchants, and Syrian caravans passing through at all hours of the day and night, not to mention dozens of students like Yeshua studying at the rabbinical school. Most were young men like my son, but a few were older than me.

We lived for a month with Shimon. He was a fine man, steady as a rock indeed, and a good *friend to my son. His mother-in-law, however, was a tiresome woman forever complaining about her illnesses, real and imagined. I was thrilled when we finally got a place of our own.*

It was nothing more than a small wooden hut on the shore near the fishing boats, but there was always a cool breeze blowing across the lake. I busied myself making the place into a home and cooking for Yeshua and whatever companions he might bring home. He worked hard during the days, usually on projects on the waterfront. He became quite skilled at building boats during those years and was sought out by fishermen from around the lake. But as soon as the sun set, he would be at the school studying with the elder Pharisees, most of whom he greatly admired.

Some of my son's followers today think that he saw the Pharisees as enemies. How absurd! Yeshua was a Pharisee himself and proud of the name. Of course he argued with them, just like they did with each other. A room full of Pharisees resembles nothing so much as a yard of chickens fighting over table scraps. But at the end of the evening they would all go to the local tavern to laugh and drink wine together.

As much as he enjoyed being with the other students, Yeshua's closest friends were the farmers and fishermen he met every day. Shimon was chief among them, but also his brother Andreas, then Yakov and his brother Yochanan—Yeshua teasingly called them the "sons of thunder" because their voices were so loud—Tau'ma, who never believed anything unless he saw it himself, and a few others, including Mattityahu, who had given up his job as a tax collector to become a student at the rabbinical school with Yeshua.

Yes, Rebekah, Yehuda the Iscariot was there too from the beginning.

They would often gather at our house in the evening or on Shabbat. Yeshua shared with them what he had studied that day, but in language and stories they could easily understand. It seemed our home was always filled with people Yeshua had befriended. One day he even brought home an old leper—into my house!— who he had found on the edge of town. Yeshua gave him some food and a jug of wine, then sent him on his way with a kiss. I told him he was never to do such a thing again.

After a few years in Kefar Nahum, Yeshua began to travel around Galilee for several weeks at a time with his friends. There were many like him then, itinerant rabbis who would teach in the village marketplaces or under a fig tree. On Shabbat he would read the Torah in services if called on and preach at the local synagogue if the town had one. Sometimes he would be asked to pray over a sick person, which he always did reluctantly. It wasn't that he didn't want to help people, but he wanted his ministry to be one of teaching.

What did he teach? You already know, Rebekah. You've heard the stories since you were a little girl. You met Shimon, Yochanan, and the others and listened to them tell the tales of those early days. I won't repeat what is known well enough already. Today the stories of my son are told throughout the world, from Judea to Babylon and even, I hear, in Rome. I have no secret knowledge to pass on to you or anyone. Like every other Pharisee, Yeshua taught the law and the prophets and urged people to love each other and draw close to the Almighty. He even taught us to love our enemies—that was something I never heard the other rabbis say—though I must admit it is a lesson I still struggle to learn.

What few people seem to remember are the women. Yeshua offended many during those years by his friendship with women of all sorts. He treated them as equals and listened carefully to all they had to say. Even Shimon would sometimes warn him that he was endangering all that he wanted to do by allowing women such an important role in his ministry. The Pharisees are talking, his friends would say. But Yeshua would always laugh and say that's what Pharisees do best.

Chief among the women was Miryam from the town of Magdala on the lake just south of Kefar Nahum.

Of course you know all about her, Rebekah. She was your mother. But I speak of her for those who will come after.

She was a rich young widow whose husband had been a prosperous merchant trading in fish sauce. Even the most conservative Pharisees treated her with great respect since she was an important patroness and made frequent donations to the rabbinical school. She was about the same age as my Yeshua and I often thought she would have made him a fine wife. They would talk for hours by the lake, but there was never any hint of impropriety or scandal—not that a few people didn't whisper about them. When Yeshua began his ministry around Galilee, she and her female companions would often accompany him and his friends. They weren't servants, but partners, helping to organize the gatherings, buying and preparing food for the crowds, bringing people to hear my son, and teaching among the women of the towns. And it goes without saying that Miryam's money made it all possible. Without her support, Yeshua would be forgotten today.

I remember a story about your mother, Rebekah. I suppose you're old enough to know. You're a grown woman yourself now and can look at your mother as a woman too.

Yeshua had taken just a few of his followers, including Miryam, with him when he went to the Phoenician city of Tyre on the coast north of Galilee. He had gone to preach there among the Jews of the city. But after he received a poor reception at the synagogue, he went to the marketplace and spoke to Greeks in their own language, preaching words of kindness and charity that gained approval from many in the crowd. The Jewish leaders were scandalized and drove him out of town.

Yeshua and his friends went to the seashore after that and stayed at an inn by the water. None of them had ever seen the sea before. They were amazed at how it stretched beyond the horizon.

Your mother told me years later about that night when she and Yeshua were sitting on the beach after the others had gone to bed.

"What do you think happens after we die?" she asked him.

"Why? Are you planning on dying soon?"

"Don't be difficult, Yeshua. You rabbis love to answer a question with another question. I think you do it to be annoying. You know I'm just curious what you think."

"Well, Miryam, what do the scriptures say?"

"You're doing it again, Yeshua." She sighed.

He laughed. "It's what they taught us at the rabbinical school. But to answer your question, Miryam, I think we go to be with the Almighty."

"That's not much of an answer," she replied. "Go where? What's it like there?"

"I don't know," he replied. "I haven't died yet."

"But surely you must have some ideas."

"Well, some people say it's a place of judgment. Some think it's an endless banquet. Others say that it's a place of pure light and joy."

"But what do you think, Yeshua?"

"I think, Miryam, that it's impossible for us to know what our lives after this one will be like. I think it lies beyond our imagination, as it should. If we knew what happened after death, we wouldn't think about our lives here in this world. We would spend all our days imagining what it's like for those we loved who have died or what it will be like for us. That would be a terrible waste of life. This is the world the Almighty has given us for now, for ourselves and for our children. This is the world we must live in and try to heal."

They were silent for a while after that, listening to the waves lap against the shore.

"Do you ever wish you had children, Miryam?" he asked.

"Of course I do. I wish my husband had lived long enough to give me a child. He died barely a year after we were married."

"You're still young enough to have children," he said. "I don't think you'd have any trouble finding a man. You have plenty of money. And, well, you're very beautiful."

"Yeshua, are you asking me something?"

My son took her hand then. "Miryam, if I could marry any woman in the world, it would be you—if you would have me. But I can't ask you to be my wife. It wouldn't be fair to you. My life isn't going to be home and hearth. I have a job to do and it may cost me everything in the end."

"Yeshua, don't you think you should let a woman decide for herself if she's willing to share her life with you?"

"I . . . well, I suppose. But it isn't that simple, Miryam."

"You mean it's too complicated for a woman to understand?"

"Now you're the one being difficult," he said. "You know I have nothing but respect for you and the other women. What I mean is that I don't want to hurt anyone, especially you."

They sat for a while longer in the darkness.

"Would you marry me if I asked you?" he said at last.

She leaned over and kissed him. "No, Yeshua, I wouldn't."

"But why? I thought you said I should let you decide."

"And I just did."

"I don't understand. Do you . . . care about me?"

"Oh, Yeshua. I care about you more than you can imagine. You're the best man I know. I love you and would be happy to be your wife."

"Then why don't you want to marry me?"

"First of all, you didn't ask me. You asked me what I would say if you asked me. If you're going to propose to a woman, you have to have the courage to actually come out and do it. Second, and more important, you have a job to do, like you said. If I married you, you would put me and our children above everything else, even your ministry. That's the kind of man you are. I know you have a mission, Yeshua. That mission is important, more important than me. I want to do everything to help you carry it out. *That's why I won't be your wife. I won't marry you because I love you."*

Yeshua was silent again. *"Women are very hard to understand,"* he said at last.

"Yes, we are. Now it's time for you to go to bed, Yeshua. You've got to get an early start healing the world tomorrow."

She was a remarkable woman, Rebekah. But there were other women among the followers of my son aside from your mother. Two of the most important were another Miryam and Martha, sisters of El'azar or Lazarus, from the town of Bethany just outside Jerusalem.

Lazarus was a rich caravan merchant who imported incense from Arabia and had made a fortune in the booming market for frankincense and myrrh. He was an important financial supporter of several schools of the Pharisees in Jerusalem and made generous donations each year to the temple. Yeshua had met him and his sisters one summer when they had come to visit the school at Kefar Nahum, which wasn't far from an estate they owned on the lake. All the rabbis and teachers were making a terrible fuss over Lazarus and his sisters in the hope that they would donate generously to the school. But Lazarus noticed Yeshua standing in the back of the courtyard and called him forward.

"Why aren't you after my money as well?" Lazarus joked.

"I don't need it," Yeshua said pleasantly, "and neither does the school."

The Pharisees were aghast and immediately started pushing Yeshua away, saying he didn't know what he was talking about. But Miryam and Martha were intrigued.

"What should we do with our money then, young rabbi?" Martha asked Yeshua.

"Give it to the poor," he answered.

At that point the Pharisees practically threw Yeshua out of the building. But the sisters came to our house later that evening, seeking him. I was so embarrassed to have such fine people in our small hut, but they were gracious and thanked me kindly for the weak wine I poured them. They sat with Yeshua until late that night talking about the work that he might accomplish in our land. From that day forward, the sisters were among the most faithful followers of my son. They would visit often when they were in Galilee and Yeshua stayed with them several times over the next few years when he went to Jerusalem for Passover, celebrating the Seder with them at their home.

But don't think that all the women who followed Yeshua were wealthy, Rebekah. Far from it. Several were poor widows without grown sons who had lost their farms when their husbands had died. They struggled to make a living sorting fish on the shore and hiring out as mourners at funerals. A few of the them worked as prostitutes among the Greeks and Syrians of the town just to feed their children, though Yeshua tried to help them find a new life and means of support. One colorful follower was a Samaritan woman Yeshua had once met at a well on the way back to Galilee from Jerusalem. She was a large and garrulous woman who had been married more times than I could count. She settled in Kefar Nahum to run a tavern. Yeshua and his friends often met there.

You want to know about the wedding, Rebekah? Why does everyone ask me about that day? All right, I'll tell you, but let this be the end of it.

It was late spring and we had gone up from Kefar Nahum to Cana in the hills to the west of the lake. The bride was a daughter of a dear cousin of mine who was marrying a rich olive merchant from the same town. Yeshua had been invited to perform the ceremony, so he came along with his friends, including Shimon and your mother, who also was a friend of the groom's family.

The wedding was lovely. I saw family there I hadn't seen for several years, including my sister and her daughter with the twins, who were now running around the courtyard with the other children. But soon I noticed that the bride's mother was in a panic, so I asked what was wrong. She said the steward they had hired for the banquet hadn't ordered enough wine for the crowd that had gathered there. It was going to bring shame to her household on this happiest of days if they ran out. The poor woman was beside herself.

I went to see Yeshua. He was standing near the table of food with Shimon, who could eat more than any man I had ever met. I called my son aside and told him the problem.

"Well, what do you want me to do?" he asked.

"Help them, Yeshua. They're family."

"I don't have any jars of wine hidden under my cloak," he said.

By now I was getting perturbed at him and he knew it.

"Yeshua, son of Yosef, I know who you are and what you can do if you want to. I'm not asking you to part the Red Sea like Moshe, just help your own kin."

"Mother . . . ," he said, rolling his eyes.

"Don't 'Mother' me, young man. Just do something!"

I walked away and told the servants to do whatever he ordered them.

There were several large stone jars in the courtyard for purification. Yeshua looked at me pleadingly one last time, but I shook my head at him. He told the servants to fill the jars with water, then take some in a cup to the master of the feast. The servants thought this a strange command but did it anyway. Who were they to argue with a rabbi?

When the master tasted the water, he called the bridegroom over and slapped him on the back.

"Excellent wine, my boy. Most grooms serve the best wine first and the poorer stuff after the guests are all drunk, but you saved the best for last!"

Only the servants knew what had happened— but have you ever known a servant who could keep a secret? By the end of the feast everyone was talking about the miracle that Yeshua had performed. He left immediately and went back to Kefar Nahum alone. He would barely talk to me for a week after I returned. I know, I shouldn't have made him do it. He didn't want the attention and he didn't want to be known as a miracle worker. For the rest of his ministry, people kept asking him to make wine for them like they had heard he had done at Cana. But it was for his own family after all. A mother shouldn't ask her own son to help family?

There are so many stories, Rebekah. I told you I wouldn't repeat what you already know, but there is one last tale I want to tell you. I think about it often, because I believe it was the beginning of the end for Yeshua.

We were in Jerusalem for Passover. I usually didn't travel so far with Yeshua, but I wanted to see the temple again and stand before the house of the Almighty. Say what you will about King Herod—and I could say many terrible things—the man could build, and the temple was his most magnificent creation.

Yeshua and I were staying at the home of Lazarus near the Mount of Olives. He liked to rise early in the morning when we were there and walk among the ancient trees. That morning I went with him. It was such a peaceful place. You could see the temple across the Kidron Valley gleaming in the rising sun and hear the priests busily preparing for the sacrifices.

Yeshua had been teaching in the temple court-yard during the previous few days. The priests and Pharisees of Jerusalem were not happy with the crowds he was starting to gather around him. They were nervous, with good reason, that the

Roman soldiers in the nearby Fortress of Antonia would see any massing of people as the start of an insurrection. Just two days before, there had been trouble and bloodshed when a rabbi from Cyrene had called on the Jews to rise up against the occupation of the land and the violation of their sacred temple. Everyone knew it wouldn't take more than a small spark to start a fire that would consume us all.

That morning Yeshua seemed distracted and sadder than I had seen him in a long time.

"What are you thinking about, my son?" I asked him.

"Nothing. Everything," he said.

"If you don't want to talk, just tell me," I said. "I won't bother you."

He smiled at me.

"It's not that, Mother. I was thinking of all that's happened in this place over the centuries and all that will in the ages to come. Nothing lasts forever, you know. The temple that Herod built will fall someday and the people of Yisrael will be scattered to the ends of the earth."

"Are you a prophet now, Yeshua?"

"If I am, I'm in the line of Jeremiah. No one listened to him either." He took my arm. "Come on. Let's go across to the temple before the others get up. It will be an outing, just the two of us."

Of course it was never just the two of us. As soon as we reached the women's courtyard of the temple, someone recognized him from the days before and began to ask him questions. Soon a small crowd was gathered around listening to him teach. I could see the Pharisees on the edge of the crowd growing nervous and glancing up at the towers of the Roman fortress looming over the courtyard.

After half an hour or so, I heard a commotion in the back of the crowd and saw a small group of Pharisees dragging a young woman dressed in rags toward Yeshua. She looked terrified. I knew before they spoke what they were going to do. It was a trap, and a clever one at that.

They threw the woman at his feet.

"Rabbi Yeshua, we caught this woman yesterday in the very act of adultery. She was found in bed with a man not her husband and we have witnesses. The law of the Almighty says that she should be stoned to death. What do you say?"

Stoning for adultery was rare in Jerusalem. Few there wanted to see a person suffer such a horrible fate. Usually a rabbinical court would quietly force a woman—and it was always the woman—to divorce her husband, a kind of death sentence in itself in a land where a woman alone and shunned would likely starve.

The Pharisees knew that the heart of my son's teaching was compassion and forgiveness, but that he also preached upholding the law of the Almighty. They wanted to catch him in a contradiction. If he said the woman should be forgiven, then he denied the authority of the law. If he said she should be stoned, his message of compassion would ring hollow throughout the land.

I looked at the frightened woman at Yeshua's feet and remembered that day years before when I had knelt naked in the marketplace of Nazareth waiting for the stones to fall on me. I wanted to say something to my son, to tell him that could be his own mother in the dirt, that it could be any woman in this world.

But instead of arguing with the Pharisees, Yeshua bent down and began to write in the dust with his finger. He didn't even look at them as he traced in the dirt each of their names.

They began to be afraid. Yeshua continued to write. Now, beside each of their names, he wrote their most secret sins, the dark transgressions they most wanted to hide from the world.

Without glancing at them, he said: "Kill her then. But let whoever among you is without sin cast the first stone."

He continued to write in the dirt as they slowly walked away, ashen and ashamed. After a few minutes he looked up and saw they had all gone. He knelt and helped the woman to her feet, then wiped away her tears. He looked at the crowd, then at her as he spoke:

"Who condemns you now?"

"No . . . no one . . . sir," she stammered.

"Then neither do I," he said. "Go and sin no more."

The woman kissed his hands, then left. The crowd dispersed in silence.

When it was just the two of us remaining, Yeshua took his sandaled foot and smoothed out the words he had written in the dirt until they were gone.

He took my hand then, something he hadn't done since he was a little boy, and we walked out of the courtyard without a word.

Chapter Fifteen

I was about to unroll the scroll to reveal a new column when Olwen burst into the room.

"You've got to leave, now! Gather your things quickly and follow me."

The look on her face told me what was happening.

"They're coming," she said. "I don't know how they found you so fast. Three ships from the south with black sails full of men with swords. Two more ships waiting on the far shore. Something terrible is about to happen. We don't have much time."

I rolled up the scroll and put it back into the case while Dari threw our things into the satchels. Olwen added some bread she had brought from the dining hall. We were out of the room in less than a minute.

Olwen led us out of the front door of the main building and beyond to the gate of the garden. The abbess was standing there with the other sisters gazing out onto the bay at the ships. They were large sailing vessels, not just fishing curraghs, and I could see the glint of swords in the sun even at this distance. There must have been a dozen men on each ship. The two outlaw ships still on the shore were equal in size. They were probably holding back to pursue us in case we tried to flee the island.

Next to the ships on the beach I saw two wooden posts with someone tied to each. I could tell both were women by the dresses they wore, but they were too far away to recognize faces. The larger figure was motionless and slumped over, but the smaller one was writhing and screaming. One of the outlaws went to her and her head fell forward, then the front of her dress was covered in red.

Dear God, they had cut her throat just for taking us across to the island. Her mother was surely dead as well. They were innocent and had both died because of me.

I turned back in tears to the sisters gathered near me. Even with death bearing down on them, they didn't look afraid. They had seen what happened to the women on shore, but they didn't move. They watched the approaching boats with a look of determination and, oddly I thought, pity.

"Deirdre," the abbess said sternly, "you and Dari follow Olwen to the north side of the island. We have a fast boat there you can take across to the mainland. Olwen will sail back here while you escape inland. Wherever you go, travel quickly and get as far as you can away from here. They will surely follow you."

"But Mother," I said, "we can't just leave you to face these men alone. You've got to escape too. I recognize those sails. They're Lorcan's men. Those outlaws will kill every one of you."

Lorcan was a ruthless outlaw based on Lambay Island off the eastern coast. I had encountered him briefly once before and had barely escaped with my life. He controlled virtually every nefarious activity in Ireland, from cattle thievery to slave raiding. I couldn't believe Bartholomew would hire a man as vicious as Lorcan to come after us. I had underestimated how determined the monk was.

The abbess put her hand on my shoulder. "Don't worry about us. We have a few tricks in our basket. Just get Dari and yourself to safety. And finish translating that scroll. Go now."

Olwen took us both by our sleeves and pulled us away from the sisters, who were forming a circle and starting to sing together. I thought they must be out of their minds. I wanted to rush back and make them listen to me, but Olwen and now Dari were dragging me away. As we climbed the path over the hill that led to the north side of the island, I looked back and saw that they had raised their hands to the sky and were singing ever more loudly. But this music wasn't like what I heard in the worship hall the night before. It was dark and discordant, with rhythms and tones that sent shivers down my spine.

Why weren't they running away? Did they really think singing would save them? Didn't they know they were all about to die? I didn't want anyone else to sacrifice their lives for me.

But then I looked up. What had just a few minutes ago been a bright blue sky had suddenly grown dark. There was a wind stirring around us and low gray clouds were racing swiftly in the air as we climbed the hill. Lightning flashed and thunder echoed across the island. Rain began to fall in torrents. It seemed as if the forces of nature herself were gathering above our heads. All the while the sisters kept singing.

Suddenly the storm moved out from the island into the bay toward the ships. I could see the white tops of waves striking them and pouring over the sides. One of the black sails was ripped away from its mast, while the men in the other two boats struggled to lower their own sails. I saw them trying in vain to turn the ships back to the men on shore and heard their cries across the water as they called to their gods for help.

Then from the deep ocean out of the west, I saw an immense wave moving toward the ships. Dari and I stood on the crest of the hill in wonder and horror as we heard the men scream and watched the massive wave, now taller than an oak tree, overtake the boats and drive them down to the depths of the sea.

As soon as they had come, the wave and storm disappeared. The wind suddenly ceased and the clouds began to move away. The sun came out once again. I looked to the now calm bay for survivors or at least bodies, but there was nothing. Every scrap of wood, every man on the ships was simply gone.

The men on the shore stood staring at the water. Their own ships were battered but unharmed.

The sisters far below us ended their song and lowered their arms. They then walked slowly and, it seemed, with great sorrow, back through the garden gate and into the monastery.

Olwen was crying, but she urged us over the hill and down the path to the shore.

"We've got to move fast," she said. "The other men won't be stunned for long—and they will be angry. They will have seen us on the hill and figured out where we're going. They'll sail around the bay to the northern shore before we can get there if we don't hurry."

"Olwen, how in the name of heaven did the sisters do that?" Dari asked. "It was amazing."

"No, Dari," she said, shaking her head. "It wasn't amazing, it was terrible. The end of any life, even the lives of those who would harm us, is a tragedy for us all."

"I'm so sorry," I said. "It's because of us those men are dead. We're the ones who made you do that."

"You didn't make us do anything, Deirdre," she shouted back at us as we all ran down the path to the shore. "We welcomed you into our monastery knowing what was going to happen, we just didn't think it would happen so soon. The task you've been given is a great one. You must finish it. But you're no longer safe on this island. We can't keep doing what you saw. It takes too much from our spirits. You must find another place to finish your work."

At a rocky cove on the northern shore of the island, we found the promised boat pulled up high on the beach. It was a longer and narrower version of the curragh we had crossed in the previous day with a large white sail hanging limply from the mast. The three of us hauled it into the water, then we climbed in and raised the sail. There was a steady breeze from the south that sped us swiftly out into the bay. We knew that the men watching from the southern coast would see us leaving the island and come after us, though they would probably stay close to shore, fearing the sisters would stir up another storm. We pulled away eastward toward the dark forests beneath the mountains on the mainland. In less than an hour, we felt the bottom of the ship scraping the rocks of the shore.

I could see two black sails moving around the bay heading toward us. We had maybe an hour before they reached us.

Dari and I jumped out and made a quick farewell to Olwen, who was already turning the boat back to the island.

"Go in peace," she shouted, "but go quickly!"

We ran into the forest on the near side of a small river flowing out of the heights above us. Neither Dari nor I was a stranger to moving fast when necessary. We put our endurance to the test that afternoon as we climbed swiftly through the trees and up into the mountains.

"Deirdre, do you think the sisters on the island will be all right?"

"I don't know. I hope so. Lorcan's men will want revenge against them, but they'll also be afraid, with good reason."

When at last evening drew near and we had reached the summit of the highest peak, I looked back across the bay toward the setting sun. I could see Clare Island in the distance. I could also see the two black ships far below at the beach where we had landed. Lorcan's men were already tracking us inland. Dari and I quickly drank cold water from a mountain stream, then ate a little of the bread Olwen had given us. We fought our aching muscles and ran on into the night.

By late the next morning we were on the northern shore of Lough Conn, a large blue lake nestled in the hills west of the River Moy. I found a small cave in the hillside and chased a family of angry badgers out of it before covering the entrance with branches. Once inside, Dari and I had a little more bread and dared to sleep for a couple of hours.

I had traveled this corner of Ireland before and knew there were few farms in these hills. The only people who lived here were shepherds grazing their flocks. Nearby was the small settlement where Patrick himself had been held as a slave decades before, but that had burned long ago and was deserted. Still, I wasn't going near any farms, empty or not. We were going to stay deep in the forests and travel by night until we were far from the western coast.

We reached the River Moy that night and walked in the freezing water for miles to throw off the men tracking us. Then we climbed up a barren ridge of the Ox Mountains to the headwaters of a swift stream called the Owenbeg and traveled in the water again through the night. We stayed in the stream down from the hills, then again up a narrow river the next night to Lough Key and across at last to the Iron Mountains. I didn't think anyone could follow through all of that unless they had the birds of the air spying for them. When we reached those desolate peaks in the early afternoon, I built a small fire in a hidden valley and roasted some fish we had caught by hand along the way. I had never felt so exhausted in my life.

"We're as far away from the sea as we can get," Dari said. "Does anybody live in this terrible place? I don't know about you, but I'm desperate for some real sleep. Maybe we could make camp for a day to rest and finish translating the scroll. Once we're done we could go back to Kildare and be done with it."

"I doubt it will be that simple, but I agree we've got to finish translating the gospel quickly. The longer we have it, the greater the danger we're in. But we don't have to sleep under a rock. There is one person who lives in these mountains, if she's still alive, and we might be able to stay with her. I don't think Lorcan's men will find her. I'm not even sure I can."

"Who is she?"

"Follow me and I'll show you."

We made our way eastward a few miles up the dark valley through thick brambles and scrawny haw-thorn bushes deep into the mountains. Just when Dari thought I was completely lost, we came at last to a jagged rock as tall as three men standing away from the side of a barren cliff. The headwaters of the stream we had followed led away from a crack behind the rock barely big enough for us to squeeze through. The far end the black cavern opened up to a space the size of a small chapel. The sun pouring in from above through an opening high in the rock reflected off the water and made the light dance in shifting patterns across the stone. In the corner of the cave was a wall of unworked granite rocks built into the face of the cliff with a thatch roof laid out over it. A thin column of smoke from a cooking fire wound its way up the side of the cliff but faded away before it could reach the open sky far above our heads.

"Who lives here, Deirdre?"

"A very special woman. Let me do the talking."

I went to the side of the stone hut where a mottled gray cloth serving as a door hung just a few feet above the ground. You would have sworn it was part of the rock until you touched it.

"Prudentia, it's me, Deirdre. Please don't be afraid."

Nothing happened at first, then finally a single eye peeked around the edge of the cloth.

"It's all right, Pru. It's only me and my friend Dari. She's a sister at Brigid's monastery as well. If you let us in, I'll explain everything."

The single eye looked at me for a moment more, then moved to Dari who had come to stand behind me.

I had met Prudentia years before when Brigid was still alive, before I was a nun. I had been planning a trip from my grandmother's house in Kildare to a farm in Ulster to sing at a wedding. Brigid had said she wanted to visit an old friend in the Iron Mountains and wondered if I wanted some company for part of the journey. I was honored to have her join me and enjoyed her company for the few days we walked north through the fields covered with spring flowers. Brigid was a gifted storyteller and told me as we traveled of the woman she was going to meet.

Prudentia was what Father Ailbe called a voluntary mute. Sometimes these were people of great holiness who had taken a vow of silence to draw closer to God. But in Prudentia's case it was the result of trauma she had suffered long ago. From that point on she communicated with her rare visitors solely by writing on a wax tablet.

Over fifty years earlier when Brigid was still a young nun looking for a place to establish her monastery, she had taken a shortcut through these mountains in winter when she broke her leg in a fall, leaving her at the mercy of the wolf packs that frequented these isolated peaks. Unable to move and freezing to death, Prudentia heard her singing hymns and helped her back to her cave. There she nursed Brigid to health over the next few weeks until she could walk out of the mountains on her own.

Prudentia had been kidnapped from western Britain as a teenager. She was brought to Ireland by raiders and sold to a local farmer, just as Patrick was. Her master and his sons abused her terribly and beat her brutally when she stopped speaking. When she was about twenty years old, she ran away from their farm and took refuge in the Iron Mountains—a place so hostile to human life that not even her former owner would dare to follow her there. And so she had lived alone in this cavern ever since.

Prudentia at last pulled back the curtain and held it open for us to enter. Her hut was small even for one person. The cliff face formed one wall against which her short wooden bed was placed, covered in a thick pile of woolen blankets. A stone hearth was next to it with a small iron pot hanging over the fire. It smelled like she was cooking a fish stew, which I realized must be almost all she ate since she had no cow or chickens, though I did see a few wild bird eggs on the single shelf above her bed. There were also several books there, including a copy of *Passion of Perpetua and Felicity* and the Bible that Brigid had given her during our visit years earlier. Aside from these and a heavy black cloak hanging near the door, the only other objects in the hut were dozens of woven reed crosses scattered about. These were the same ancient icons of the Irish sun goddess that Brigid had used in her teaching, turning them effortlessly, as she did with so many things, from signs of the old religion into symbols of the new faith.

When I had seen Prudentia over a decade earlier I thought she had looked ancient, but now she seemed like Methuselah's grandmother. I knew she must be at least a century old. She was bent almost double with age and her skin was practically transparent as it often is in the very elderly. Her fine white hair was braided far down her back, while the shawl over her shoulders could barely disguise that she was more bones than flesh. But her blue eyes were as bright as ever, though still haunted by the fear she had carried since she was a girl.

She motioned for Dari and me to sit down on the bed, then slowly ladled steaming fish stew into a single wooden bowl for us to share. She stood in the corner of her hut away from us and watched us eat. When we were done, she took the bowl and went to the shelf to search for her wax tablet and stylus. Her hands were arthritic and cramped, but her writing was clear:

Why are you here?

I told her the story from the beginning until we arrived in the Iron Mountains. She listened carefully, though looking away, and met my eyes only once when I mentioned who the author of the gospel might be.

When I was done she smoothed out the wax with the blunt end of the stylus and wrote again:

Stay and work.

"Thank you, Pru. I don't think our pursuers will find us here. I covered our tracks well. We only need another day to finish, then we'll be gone."

She nodded, then spread some of her blankets on the dirt floor in front of the fire for Dari and me. The sun had set outside the cave and the only light was the soft glow of the fire. I didn't see any candles or a lamp about. I had a feeling Prudentia was so familiar with her simple home and its surroundings that she could function in darkness just as well as day. When Dari and I had settled on the blankets Prudentia took two of her reed crosses from the wall and handed them to us.

"We shouldn't take these from you, Pru."

She ignored me and with great difficulty knelt beside us by the fire. She closed her eyes and prayed, moving her lips but not making a sound as we prayed silently with her. Then she struggled back to her feet and across to her bed where she lay down with her back turned to us.

"I feel like I'm visiting one of the spirits of our ancestors," Dari whispered to me.

"I know what you mean. She's kind to help us, but I know it's hard for her to have anyone around. We should start early tomorrow and finish the translation so we can be gone before sunset."

"We'll have to work outside. There's not enough light in this cave."

"That should be all right. It doesn't look like rain."

"Do you really think we lost Lorcan's men?"

"Yes. I wouldn't have risked coming here if I thought they could track us. I won't put Pru or anyone else in danger because of me. We just have to figure out a way to get back to Kildare and inside the walls of the monastery when we're done. We should be safe if we can do that, at least for a while."

"I hope so. I'm tired of running."

"Me too. Sleep well, Dari. We've got to finish translating the gospel tomorrow."

Chapter Sixteen

N ot that last week, Rebekah.
No.
I don't want to remember it.

"That's odd."

"What?" Dari asked. We were sitting on two low rocks in the early morning sun by the stream outside of Prudentia's cave. She had risen even earlier than us and had tottered into the mountains with a basket for holding the fish she somehow caught.

"The scroll breaks off here. There's a gap, then it starts again below."

"Why would the scribe do that?"

"I don't know. It's not a large gap, just enough for a few lines, then it begins again in the same hand. But . . . there's something here."

I held the scroll up to the sun. The writing was always hard to read, but the letters I could see in the gap were barely visible. They had been written on the papyrus, then partially washed away.

"There are words here."

The end of the story of Miryam, mother of Yeshua of Nazareth. May it be a blessing to all who read it. Written by the hand of Rebekah, daughter of Miryam of Magdala.

"That's it?" Dari asked.

"Yes. It looks like our speaker wanted to stop, so the scribe wrote a coda, an ending, but then she started again after the speaker decided to continue."

"If it was too painful for Mary to continue at first, I wonder what changed her mind?"

"There's only one way to find out."

Sit, Rebekah, and take up your stylus again. But first, burn the last of the frankincense for me. I don't want the Romans to have it. It's all that remains of a gift from long ago. It reminds me of my Yeshua.

It's over.

We just received word.

Jerusalem has fallen.

Sacrifices have ceased for the first time in centuries and the temple has been burned to the ground, just like Yeshua said it would be. The priests have been executed and the zealots crushed. The Romans have killed tens of thousands, including women and children they deemed unfit to sell into slavery. The city is bathed in blood.

The Romans will surely come here soon and destroy all we have built. You and the others must go. No, I'm not leaving. I'm too old to run. They killed Yosef and Yeshua. Let them kill me too. I have seen enough of life.

But I will finish my story for your sake and for those who come after us.

All the world knows what happened in Jerusalem over forty years ago when my son went there for the last time. Others have told the story and they have told it well enough. Shimon, Yochanan, Mattityahu, and the rest. Even Saul from Tarsus spread the tale across the lands of the goyim before the Romans killed him, as they did Shimon soon after. Why do they destroy everything they touch? Why did the Almighty create such a race? Yeshua would say there was a reason for it all, but I cannot see it.

All I can tell you is my story of that last week, a mother's story.

We arrived in Bethany to celebrate the Passover at the home of Lazarus. I had warned Yeshua not to go into the city, but he wouldn't listen to me. What son listens to his mother? Everyone knew that since he had shamed the Pharisees in the temple during his last visit they wanted to kill him. Yes, they were afraid he would bring down the wrath of the Romans on us all, but their hatred was also personal. Not all of them, of course. There were many Pharisees and even some members of the Sanhedrin who admired my son and took his teachings into their hearts. Nicodemus and Yosef from Arimathea were among them, may the Almighty bring rest to their spirits. But most were afraid of the priests and the powerful Pharisees of Jerusalem who worked with them.

Lazarus gave a dinner for Yeshua and his friends at his house when we arrived. Shimon and the rest were there, including your mother. My sister had traveled with us from Galilee as well. Yehuda the Iscariot was there too, as you know.

People say many things now about Yehuda. They claim he was a demon or Satan the Adversary himself. He was none of those things. He had come to Kefar Nahum from Kerioth in the south at about the same time Yeshua and I moved there. His father had died and his family had lost their farm, like so many others. He brought his mother north to Galilee to start a new life. He had a head for numbers and worked for a prosperous perfume merchant keeping tally of his sales. He was a good son and worked hard to care for his mother, a fine woman I came to know well during our years there. Yehuda was a devoted friend and follower of my son until the day he betrayed him. You ask why he did it, Rebekah? The answer is simple: I don't know. I have asked myself that question for years. I have tried to look back into my memories and find some change in him, something that made him trade my son for silver. But I have nothing. The hearts of men are known only to the Almighty.

At the end of the dinner of Lazarus that evening, his sister Miryam took a small jar of pure nard—an aromatic oil imported all the way from India—and anointed Yeshua's feet with it. Then she wiped his feet with her hair. The rich fragrance filled the room. I was shocked, as was everyone else. It was an act of both intimacy and shameful extravagance.

Yehuda spoke for all of us when he said that this was not right. Such a jar, he said, was worth *almost as much as a man could earn in a year. It could have been sold and given to the poor.*

Yeshua told him that the poor were always among us to receive our help, but Miryam had done this act of kindness this evening in preparation for his own burial.

The room erupted at these words and everyone was shouting at him, demanding to know what he meant. I was too upset to speak. Everyone was angry at Yeshua that night, including me.

Later that evening when things had quieted down and the guests had all left, I went to find Yeshua. He was standing on the roof of the house looking at the stars. A cool breeze was blowing from the west.

"They look like thousands of campfires in the sky, don't they, Mother?"

"I don't want to talk about the stars, Yeshua. What did you mean earlier about preparing for your death? Everyone is frightened enough for you without you saying things like that to upset them."

He sighed deeply and sat down on roof. I had never seen him look so weary.

"It's time, Mother."

"Time for what, Yeshua?"

"You know what I'm talking about, Mother. You've always known."

I began to shake and my knees gave way. I sat down beside him, unable to speak.

"I'm so sorry, Mother. This isn't fair to you." Tears were rolling down his cheeks as he looked at me. *"It's what I was born to do. I don't want to die, believe me. I love the beauty of this world. I enjoy being with my friends. I wish I could go on living. I wish I could have a wife and children to grow old with. And I wish I could be with you."*

I found my voice at last. "Then be with me, Yeshua! You said you'd never leave me. You don't have to die. What are you thinking? Do you want to be some kind of sacrifice for the Passover? You think your death can save us from the Romans?"

He shook his head. "The Romans aren't the problem, Mother. Our enemy is inside of each of us. I want to change that. I want to make all things new."

"Yeshua, I don't care about saving the world. When the messenger of the Almighty came to me years ago, he didn't say anything about you dying. I won't stand by and watch you do that, do you understand me?"

"When the messenger came, Mother, you said you were the servant of the Almighty. Servants obey."

I stood up and pointed my finger in his face. "Not this time, young man. If the Almighty wants you to die, I won't be there to watch. He asks too much! I will curse the day he chose you for this. And I will curse him!"

"You don't mean that, Mother. I know you don't. I need your strength for what's coming. Please don't leave me. I promise, it will be all right."

He stood up and held me tightly.

I felt his tears on my robe. What could I do? I embraced him in return and comforted him as best I could, just as when he was a child.

I saw him very little that next week. He was often away at the temple preaching to the crowds. He came back to the house of Lazarus at night and we would talk, but never about death. We spoke of the old days when Yosef was still alive. We talked of all the joys we had shared as a family. We laughed together and remembered friends and family we had loved.

On that last night before he left for the garden with Shimon and the others, I kissed him farewell. I could barely see because of my tears. We both knew he would not be coming back.

He kissed me as well and held me for a long time before he spoke. "It will be all right, Mother. I meant it when I said I would never leave you. Please believe that. And I will love you, always."

"I believe you, Yeshua. I love you too."

And then I watched him go. He had come into my life as a gift from the Almighty. Now he was gone. I knew he had never really belonged to me, but he was my son. My beloved son.

I wasn't there when they arrested him in the garden. I wasn't there when the high priest brought him before Pilate, cursed be his name. I wasn't there when they beat him so horribly that he almost died. But I was there when they brought him to the Place of the Skull, the small hill just outside the walls of Jerusalem they call Golgotha.

How can I speak of it, Rebekah? To see my own son nailed to a cross, to watch him struggle to breathe, to watch the blood drip from his body to the ground below. This was my little boy, the one I had protected when he was young. But now I could do nothing. No mother should have to endure such a thing.

Your mother was there with me, Rebekah. I don't know what I would have done without her. Yochanan was there as well standing beside me, holding me up.

At the end, Yeshua looked down at me. I don't know how he did it, he had no strength left and was in unbearable pain, but he smiled at me. The guards let me go forward to him at last. Barbarians they were, but they had mothers too.

I held his feet, covered with blood, in my hands. I called out his name. I told him I was there. He struggled to speak and at last mouthed one word to me:

"Always."

And then I watched him die.

I stayed there with him until the Romans lowered his body from the cross. As the sun began to set, I held him in my arms, kissed his face, prayed to the Almighty that I could die with him.

Yosef of Arimathea came and took his body away to be buried in his own tomb nearby. I was grateful. I followed him, along with your mother, to the grave. Yochanan had gone to tell Shimon and the others of his death.

I don't remember much about those next few days. Somehow Miryam and the other women carried me back to the house of Lazarus where I lay on a bed, numb to the world. Servants brought food and drink, but I wanted nothing.

It was the morning after Shabbat ended that your mother came to me with the news that she had seen Yeshua alive. Her words meant nothing to me. I had watched my son die. I turned my head away from her.

Shimon came the next day with Yochanan and said the same to me. I cursed them and told

them to leave me. Why were they torturing me?
Hadn't I been through enough?

It was the next night when I was lying in bed
that I heard someone in the room with me even
though the door had not opened.

I turned and saw Yeshua sitting in the chair
next to my bed.

"Are you a ghost or just a dream?" I asked
him.

"Neither, Mother," he said, smiling at me.

"I don't believe it, Yeshua. I don't believe
you're here. I'm just imagining you. Please go
away."

I turned back to face the wall and closed my
eyes. I felt a hand on my shoulder and a kiss on
my cheek.

I lay there for a long time wondering why the
Almighty was so cruel to me. Couldn't he leave
me alone? What more did he want from me?

At last I turned back to look at the chair. It
was empty.

"Yeshua?"

But there was no reply.

That was over forty years ago.

My life since then has been remembering. I
remember for myself and I remember for those
who have come to see me here at Beth-horon,
where I have lived all these years with those

women who follow the teachings of my son. It was the idea of your mother, may her soul find peace. She was the one who brought us together in this small valley. A community of women living, working, and worshipping together. Here we made a life for ourselves. We feed the poor, tend to the sick, and teach the children, just as Yeshua told us to. Some women, like you, Rebekah, have become great scribes and scholars, though the priests at Jerusalem would never have allowed you among them. Women as well as a few men who follow Yeshua have come here over the years to learn and go forth as leaders in their own lands. Saul of Tarsus came after he stopped killing followers of my Yeshua, telling me he wanted to learn more about my son. He was an arrogant man who made enemies easier than friends. I never trusted him after what he had done to our people, but he spread the teaching of Yeshua across the sea and died in Rome preaching to the broken souls in that evil city, so I suppose he was sincere. May the Almighty be with his spirit.

But most of the visitors to our community here at Beth-horon over the years have been women— Jewish and Greek—who lived beyond the land of Yisrael. Priscilla from Corinth, kind old Lois, her daughter Eunice, Lydia of Macedonia, Phoebe the merchant, and especially dear Junia the apostle—I remember them all. They were the ones who established the meeting places, usually in their own homes, for followers of my son in their cities. They gave bread to the hungry, shelter to widows and prostitutes, and hope to anyone who came to them. They organized everything—women usually do. They often led the services in which women and men stood together as equals before the Almighty. When the men in their cities were too frightened to oppose the Romans, these women stood firm. Some paid for their faith with their lives, but without them the teachings of my son would never have taken root in those distant places. That is the story everyone seems to have forgotten, Rebekah. It was women like your mother who made possible the ministry of my son while he was still alive and it was women more than men who spread his teachings across the world. If the day ever comes when someone tries to tell you otherwise, tell them they are fools and liars.

But of course the men were important too, especially the friends of Yeshua who were there from the beginning. Shimon and the rest long ago went out into the world to tell the story of my son. Yochanan offered to stay with me, but I sent him away. He wanted to preach among the Greeks. I think they call him Ioannes or John.

Whether he is still alive, I don't know. Some of Yeshua's other companions came to visit me regularly in those early years, but now they all have gone to be with the Almighty. Other men came to our village from time to time seeking me out. I talked with them and told them about Yeshua, but I had no wish to become some kind of oracle as among the Greeks. I am an old woman, nothing more.

Now my story is over.

You need to leave, Rebekah, quickly, before the Romans come. I will die soon whether they come or not. Take the scroll with you and seal it away. Perhaps someday someone will read the words and remember my Yeshua, as I do.

Always.

Chapter Seventeen

Dari and I sat silently on our rocks by the stream as the sun passed behind the mountains to the west. The shadows were growing long in the valley as evening approached and a cold wind was blowing from the north. But neither of us was ready to move or even speak.

At last Dari rolled up the parchment with her translation and placed it in its container. I still held the papyrus scroll as I looked at the final words of Mary.

I took the scroll and touched it to my lips with a prayer. Then I put it gently back into the case that had guarded it for centuries. I twisted the top onto it and placed both documents into my satchel. I stood and wrapped my arms around Dari, both of us wiping tears from our faces.

"I'm not the scholar you are," Dari said, "but I think it's genuine. If I were to imagine what Mary would say, it would be something like the words on that scroll. She talks about her life like a real woman. And there's nothing in her story that seems out of place to me. Even the episode of Jesus on the beach with Mary Magdalene doesn't seem so startling. Whatever else he was, he was a man. Men fall in love. It doesn't take away anything from Jesus that he was attracted to a woman. To me, it makes him more real, more human."

"But not everyone is going to agree with you, Dari. People have a picture of Christ in their heads that they don't want challenged."

"People need to be challenged," she said. "We get lazy in our faith when we get too comfortable. Besides, the Jesus in this gospel isn't revolutionary. I don't see how Bartholomew or anyone could object to how Mary portrays him in her stories. He's kind and loving. There's nothing in the story that makes him anything less than the Christ we worship."

"Bartholomew would say it doesn't matter," I answered. "And he's right that if we give people a new picture of Jesus, some will find ways to twist it into a perversion of Christianity. This gospel will spawn a dozen new sects, all fighting with the church and with one another. Remember, there's nothing so spiritually intoxicating as thinking that you and your little group alone follow the one true faith. People will cheerfully die for such beliefs."

"Deirdre, do you mean that you want to destroy the scroll too?"

"No, of course I don't. And to answer your question, I do think that this scroll is genuine. I believe it preserves the actual words of Mary, the mother of Jesus."

"What made you finally decide that?" she asked.

"Because there are plenty of false gospels in circulation, all trying to prove some mysterious doctrine. But this scroll isn't like that. It's simply the story of a mother's love."

"Well, assuming we can make it home to Kildare, what do we do then?"

"I think we'll be safe if we can get inside the monastery. I'm sure King Dúnlaing will post his own guards around Kildare if I ask him to. Cormac would probably send some men as well. Then we'll make dozens of copies of the gospel and send them out into the world, including to Rome. I don't know how it will turn out in the end. I don't know what it will mean for our monastery at Kildare. But I will not let down all the women who have guarded this scroll through the centuries."

Finally, as the last of the light was fading, I looked up into the mountains.

"I wonder where Prudentia is? It seems like she should have returned by now."

"Do you think we should go look for her?" Dari asked.

"I wouldn't know where to begin. She's been roaming these peaks for eighty years. She could be anywhere."

"Maybe we can help." The voice was that of a young man with long blond hair who stepped out from behind the nearest boulder. At the same time six outlaws with swords drawn appeared from above and below us. How they had managed to sneak up on us so skillfully I didn't know, but we were surrounded.

I drew my father's sword from my belt and pointed it at the young man, who was clearly the leader in spite of the fact he was a good foot shorter than any of the hulking giants with him.

"Now, now, none of that." He stepped closer with his hands raised. "There's no need for anyone to be hurt, especially not me. Why don't we all relax? We have a long journey ahead of us."

I quickly ran through my options, all of which were bleak. Dari was unarmed and there was no way we could fight our way past this crew even if she were. I looked at her and saw she was ready to follow my lead, but I shook my head. They had us and they knew it.

If we resisted, we were dead. The fact that he said we had a journey ahead of us meant they weren't going to kill us right away.

I lowered my sword.

"Smart girl." The young man came forward and took my sword and satchel with the scroll and Dari's translation. Two others bound our hands tightly behind our backs.

"How did you find us?" I asked.

"You didn't make it easy." He laughed. "We had to double back a couple of times along the rivers you waded through, but we found your tracks on the banks eventually. We're very good at this sort of thing."

"You weren't so good at Clare Island." I don't know why I was provoking him except that his smugness was getting on my nerves.

He frowned. "Those witches will get what's coming to them. The boss will see to that. Meanwhile Lorcan says we're supposed to take you to the abbot at Armagh. He said to bring you there alive if possible—but didn't say you had to be unharmed. I'll leave that part up to you. Cause me any trouble on the way or smart off to me again and I'll give you and your pretty friend here to the boys for a little fun. They play rough though, so I'd mind your manners."

The men lit torches for the journey. We weren't going to get any rest that night.

The young man grinned again. "And if you're worried about the old lady, don't be. She's not lost in the mountains."

He signaled to one of the men, who brought forward Prudentia's basket and laid it at my feet. Her head was inside staring up at me with those ancient blue eyes open wide.

Dari gasped. I started to lunge at the young man, but he held up his hand.

"Now, what did I just say about good behavior? You'll be glad to know she died well though. Didn't make a sound."

With that they shoved us forward and we began the long march to Armagh.

※

We walked northeast through the night and into the next day. About noon we stopped to eat some hard biscuits and drink water from a stream. They untied our hands only for a few minutes for the meal, then bound us again. We slept for a few hours in the rain and mud, then were roused roughly to walk again, always with at least two men in front and behind us. We were never given a chance to wash ourselves. I looked for an opportunity to escape or even to create a distraction so that Dari might run away, but the men were too clever for that. They hardly spoke at all and never to us. These outlaws were professionals doing a job without pity or sympathy. They must have captured plenty of women before who begged them to let them go. The men had learned long ago to ignore such pleas.

The routine of endless marching and short stops for food and rest went on for three days until we came at last to a hill overlooking the monastery of Armagh.

I could see the monastery clearly in the morning light below us. It was surrounded by a high outer wall of worked stone with a single gate on the eastern side. There were lower walls that served to hold sheep and cattle inside the large compound of buildings. On the southern side were a dozen or so thatched huts, with an equal number on the northern side. The impressive wooden church was at the center next to a tall bell tower. A graveyard with stone crosses spread beneath it, along with the abbot's hut next to the church. I could see the nuns' quarters and their small chapel far on the western edge of the monastery next to the pigpen.

None of the sisters of Armagh liked the abbot, but they were women who had lost their families and had nowhere else to turn or had been sold to the monastery by slave traders when they were young. They were, to a woman, devoted and kind souls dedicated to the Christian life.

There were people moving inside the walls, including several brothers in dark robes and a few nuns carrying water up from the well. I could also see a dozen or so male slaves with shaved heads laboring on a new stone building near the abbot's hut that looked like it might be a treasury.

The young leader sent one of the men running ahead to announce our arrival. When we went down the hill and through the gate, it seemed the whole monastery was there waiting for us, with the abbot and Bartholomew at the front of the crowd. The abbot was a short and stout figure with a large gold cross hanging from his neck. I would have gladly risked a beating just to knock the smile off his face.

"Well, well, Sister Deirdre and her little friend. Bound and covered in mud. Isn't this simply delicious?"

Bartholomew was standing behind him. His expression was impassive.

Our young captor handed my satchel to the abbot, who gave it in turn to Bartholomew. The monk reached inside and took out Dari's translation, glanced at the first few lines, and put it back. Then he opened the ancient case containing the gospel, removed it carefully, and held the papyrus up to the sunlight. After a moment he nodded to the abbot and put the scroll gently back into its case.

"We'll be taking our gold, abbot," said the young man. "Lorcan will be wanting his payment now that you got the women and the scroll."

"Yes, yes." He waved them away. "Follow my steward. He'll take care of you."

The sisters of Armagh stood behind the small group of monks who had gathered next to the abbot. I recognized a few from my previous visit. Some of the younger nuns started to cry.

"Quiet!" growled the abbot turning to face them. "These heretics deserve no pity—and they will get none here. Tomorrow you will all see what happens when women dare to defy the power of the church. Now everyone get back to work!"

The crowd dispersed. The abbot then gave orders to the captain of his guard.

"Take them to the empty storage house and throw them inside. Keep their hands tied—and no food or drink. I want at least four of your men around the building at all times. And, my dear Sister Deirdre, do sleep well. You'll want to be well rested for tomorrow."

The guards led us to a stone storage shed with thick walls next to the kitchen. They opened the door and pushed us inside onto the dirt floor. The small hut was empty and cold. It smelled like mold and was as dark as night. I heard a metal bolt slide against the outside of the door. I pushed myself up and stumbled around the edges of the hut, but there were no other doors and no windows. There was no escape.

"They're going to kill us, aren't they?" Dari asked. She was lying on the floor turned away from me. I sat next to her.

Dari and I hadn't had any chance to talk since the outlaws captured us. Once when we tried, one of them hit Dari in the face and left her eye bruised and swollen shut. We were both filthy and exhausted and in mourning over the loss of both the women who had died and the gospel we had worked so hard to save. It would soon be burnt, if it hadn't been already, along with Dari and myself.

"I'm sorry, Dari," I said. "This is all my fault. I should have listened to Bartholomew at Glendalough and given him the scroll then. What did I accomplish by refusing him? Maybe translating it was an act of pride on my part. That's always been my sin. I keep thinking I can change the world, but I never consider the consequences. Already three innocent women have died because of me and the sisters on Clare Island are in danger from Lorcan seeking revenge. And I don't know what will happen to our monastery at Kildare. The abbot will certainly try to use all this to persuade the bishops to shut us down, claiming we're a refuge for heretics and enemies of the church. I'm sure Bartholomew will offer him Rome's support after my defiance. With Kildare gone, the abbot's dark and angry vision of Christianity will spread across this island. Everything we've worked for—Brigid, Father Ailbe, Sister Anna—it will all come to an end because of me."

She said nothing.

"Dari, please talk to me."

"What do you want me to say, Deirdre?"

"I don't know. Something. Anything. Yell at me if you want. I can't stand your silence."

"I don't want to yell at you." She rolled over to face me. "What good would it do? It's over. But I'm not angry at you. I came with you because you're my best friend and because I believed in what we were doing. You didn't mean for anyone to die. Maybe the scroll is gone, but at least we got to hear the story of Mary, even if no one else ever will."

She struggled to sit up. "I believe in heaven, Deirdre. I don't want to die; in fact I'm terrified. But I believe there's something more than this life. I hope we can be there together."

She leaned forward and put her head against my shoulder, as I did mine against hers. We couldn't embrace with our arms tied and we were too exhausted to cry, but it was enough just to feel her touching me.

We lay back down on the floor next to each other and slept for a few hours. I had always heard that people about to die see their lives flashing in front of them and picture all the people they have loved, but instead I collapsed immediately into a dreamless sleep.

Sometime in the middle of the night, I heard the bolt on the door slide back. We sat up. When the door opened it was dark outside, but one of the guards entered with sword drawn, followed by Bartholomew with a large bag and a single candle.

"Wait outside," he said to the guard.

"But, sir, the abbot gave strict instructions . . ."

"I don't care what the abbot said. I represent the pope and the church of Rome on this island. Besides, I don't think two women pose much of threat. I'll call if I need you."

The guard left, sliding the bolt back into place.

Bartholomew looked older than he had at Glendalough. There was no joy in his face, no gloating, no pleasure in having at last accomplished the work of five centuries. He walked around behind us and untied our hands, then sat on the floor in front of us and brought a skin of wine and two loaves of bread with cheese from his bag and gave them to us. We devoured the food and shared the wine.

"I'm hoping you won't try to overpower me and escape," he said when we had finished. "If you do, there are four very large men outside who will kill you as soon as you leave this hut. There are others by the gate and on the walls."

"I know when we're beaten," I said.

"I'm sorry it turned out this way," he replied. "I never wanted any of this to happen. I never wanted anyone hurt and I certainly didn't want the two of you to die."

"Then don't kill us. As you said, you represent the pope and the church in Ireland. You've got the scroll and the translation. You won, Bartholomew. Tell the abbot to let us go. What harm can we do you now?"

"Plenty, I'm afraid. You two are the only ones who know what the scroll says. I know about the memory of a bard. You could probably recite the whole thing back to me right now."

"Then kill me and let Dari go. She's no bard. She's a schoolteacher."

"Deirdre, no," Dari said, "I'm not leaving without you."

"I'm sorry." Bartholomew shook his head. "Neither of you can leave this monastery alive. It's not just about revealing the contents of the scroll. You defied the church. If it were my choice, I might send you both away unharmed if you swore to remain silent about the gospel, but the abbot would never allow it. In the end he controls the guards here, not me. He would tie me to the stake along with you if I defied him."

He reached into his bag and brought out some rags and a skin of water. "Here. You can wash yourselves if you'd like."

"Did you read the translation, Bartholomew?"

"No."

"Why not? Are you afraid it's going to defile you?"

"No. I didn't read it because I don't want to know what it says. God has given us everything we need to know in the gospels we already have. I'm going to burn it tomorrow. I have to."

"You sound like you're trying to convince yourself of that."

"Maybe I am, but it doesn't matter. I am a loyal servant of the church."

"It's genuine, Bartholomew. It contains the words of Mary herself."

"I don't care. I told you at Glendalough, it doesn't matter."

"There's nothing that threatens the church in those pages. It's the story of a mother's love, that's all. Destroy those words and you dishonor every woman who's ever lived, including your wife and daughter. Read the gospel. You owe it to them. When you've finished, think about what they would want you to do."

We sat in silence for several minutes, then Bartholomew got up and went to the door.

"You have a couple of hours until sunrise. I'll leave you untied. You may want to spend your time praying. And please know that I will always pray for you."

The next two hours we did pray—or at least Dari prayed and I stared into the darkness. I was never good at prayer and death rushing to meet us didn't seem to make me any better at it.

Soon I heard people moving outside in the monastery yard. I couldn't tell if the sun had risen or not. After a while, the bolt on the door slid back and it opened, letting in the blinding morning sun. I hugged Dari quickly one final time. Three guards stooped and entered, bound our hands behind our backs again, and pushed us into the yard.

It seemed that everyone in the monastery was gathered there waiting for us. The brothers and priests were standing to the right with the slaves behind them. The small group of sisters were next to them with several guards watching over them. The abbot apparently wanted them to have a good view of what was about to happen. In the center of the yard was Bartholomew, with his large traveling satchel on his shoulder and my father's sword in his belt. In his hands were the scroll case and the parchment. The abbot stood next to him. In front of them was a tall stake with an enormous pile of wood stacked around it. I thought I was ready for this, but I wasn't. I felt sick to my stomach and thought I would throw up, but I forced myself to stand up straight and not look afraid. I wasn't going to give the abbot the satisfaction.

I looked at Bartholomew, but he wouldn't meet my eyes. Then I looked at Dari. I remembered the old stories of brave Christian women dying in the Roman arena for their faith. Whatever peace God had given to them, Dari had now. I envied her.

"Bartholomew, please don't do this," I pleaded one last time.

He glanced at me for a moment, then spoke to the guard standing next to the pyre. "Light the wood."

"No! Bartholomew! No!" I shouted.

"Keep her quiet," the abbot ordered.

The nearest guard stuffed a dirty rag into my mouth and tied it from behind.

"You know," said the abbot casually to Bartholomew, "it would be easier to bind them to the stake before we light the fire."

"No," replied Bartholomew, "I want them to watch the scroll burn."

"Ah, yes. There is a lovely irony in that," the abbot said with a smile.

The guards held Dari and me tightly as the flames grew. Even in the cool of the autumn morning, I could feel the tremendous heat from the fire. I tried to meet Dari's eyes, but her head was bowed in prayer. We had both seen criminals burned at the stake. It was easily the most painful of deaths and was not quick.

When the fire was roaring, Bartholomew went forward with the scroll case and Dari's parchment translation. He first took the parchment and threw it into the fire. I could see the calf skin wrinkle and burst into flames almost immediately. Then he took the ancient scroll case, held it up for all gathered there to see, and tossed it into the fire. I jerked against the grips of my guards, but they pulled me back. The words of Mary that had survived for centuries vanished in a moment.

"Now," said the abbot with a grin, "it's your turn, Sister Deirdre. Would you like to go first so you don't have to watch your friend burn? Or maybe you'd like to die together? I really don't care which you choose."

Bartholomew put his hand on the abbot's shoulder. "No one is going to die today," he said.

"What?" said the abbot.

"Let them go," said Bartholomew.

"Let them go? What are you talking about? They have to die. These two are vile heretics. They're going to burn in these flames now and for eternity in the fires of hell."

"No, they're not," Bartholomew answered calmly. "You're going to order your men to cut their bonds and they're going to walk out of this monastery with me."

The abbot stood with his mouth hanging open until he finally composed himself. "I will do no such thing! These women will die here today and I will hold you under arrest until I can send you in chains to the pope for your treachery."

"No, you won't. I hate to tell you this, abbot, but the pope doesn't like you. I rather doubt there's anyone in this world who does."

"How dare you!" he shouted. "I don't care if you or anyone *likes* me. I am the abbot of Armagh and a prince of the Uí Néill dynasty. I rule here and I will be obeyed in all things. Guards, arrest this man."

The guards looked at one another, then at the abbot, and finally at Bartholomew. They didn't know what to do.

"I said arrest him, you hulking idiots! Or do you and your families want to deal with me?"

The guards respected the power of the church and the pope, but they knew the abbot. There would be dire consequences for them, their wives, and their children if they disobeyed. They drew their swords and started toward the monk.

I had never seen a man move as swiftly and fluidly as Bartholomew did at that moment. In an instant he had pulled my sword from his belt and was holding it against the abbot's throat.

"Cut the women's cords," Bartholomew said to the guards. "Do it now or he dies."

For a moment I thought they might actually prefer that the abbot die, but then they took their knives and released us.

"What are you—" the abbot started to say. He was sweating profusely, though he was far from the fire.

"Do be quiet, abbot, " Bartholomew interrupted. "We've all heard enough from you today."

Bartholomew turned him around and put the tip of his sword against the back of the abbot's neck.

"We're going to walk out of the monastery gate now," he said to the guards. "When we get deep into the woods, I'll release your abbot there if you don't try to follow us. If you do, you'll find him dead beneath a tree. Do we all understand each other?" They nodded. "Good. Deirdre and Dari, follow me."

We walked with the abbot quickly to the wall and out of the gate.

When we had gone about a mile into the forest, Bartholomew stopped. He still held his sword against the abbot.

"Deirdre, would you mind tying him up?"

"Tie me up?" sputtered the abbot. "Why I never! I swear I'll make you pay for this, Bartholomew. I have friends in Rome, you know, powerful friends. When they hear about your atrocious treatment of me and the fact that you let these two women—"

"A gag would also be most appropriate," Bartholomew said to me.

I bound the abbot by the hands and feet rather more tightly than necessary and stuffed some rags into his mouth, then I pushed him down onto the ground beneath a tall oak tree.

"Abbot," said Bartholomew, "I strongly advise you not to send your men searching for us. You have friends in Rome, true, but so do I." He then bent down so that his face was only inches from the abbot's. "And do not trouble the sisters of Kildare in the future. You have your work and they have theirs. I will be watching you."

I knelt next to the abbot myself and tightened the cords on his hands.

"Don't worry, abbot. Your men will find you here eventually—if they bother to look for you at all. Of course, it also depends on the wolves that roam these woods. I saw some scat a little ways back that looked fresh."

His eyes grew wide and he tried to shout something at me, but the rags stopped him.

"We should go," Bartholomew said. "We need to move quickly in case the guards do come looking for him soon."

We left the abbot beneath the tree and the three of us walked south through the forest. After a few miles, we stopped by a clear stream and drank some water. Bartholomew reached into his large pack and pulled out our own satchels, some food, and my harp. He then handed me my sword.

"You should wash and change," he said. "I'll wait for you across the stream in the meadow."

When he had gone, Dari and I stripped off our old clothes and rinsed them in the stream, then bathed ourselves as best we could. When we had put on the new clothing, we waded across and found Bartholomew sitting beneath an elm tree waiting for us. We sat next to him.

"I would have built a fire and cooked some porridge," he said, "but we really shouldn't linger here. I have a feeling the abbot's men will be too afraid to leave him to die in the woods and I don't want to be nearby in case he does send them out to find us."

"Bartholomew, thank you for what you did for us. I know you're taking a huge risk. Will the pope be terribly angry at you when he finds out what happened? You know the abbot is going to send a letter and tell him everything you did."

Bartholomew leaned back against the tree and looked up at the few leaves that were still clinging to the branches above us.

"Yes, I'm sure he will. In fact, I'm counting on it. I want him to tell everyone in Rome that I burned the scroll and your translation. And I do imagine the holy father will be displeased that I threatened to kill the abbot. But I think he'll also be amused. The pope has a fine sense of humor, you know. And truly, he doesn't like that man."

"At least he'll be pleased that you destroyed the scroll," I said. "I know we were on opposite sides of this fight, but you're a good man nonetheless. I understand what duty means and I know why you feel you had to burn it."

"You're too kind, Deirdre. Kinder than I deserve."

Then he reached again into his bag. "I have a gift for you," he said.

He rummaged through the bag and at last pulled out a small leather tube. We had many like it at Kildare for storing rolled-up parchment sheets. He handed it to me.

"What is it?" I asked him.

"Look inside," he answered. "But be gentle with it."

I pulled off the top of the case and tilted it so that the contents slipped out into my hand.

It was the papyrus scroll. The gospel of Mary.

"Dear God," Dari said. "You saved it!"

"But how?" I asked. "We all saw you burn it in the fire."

"No, you saw me burn the old case and the translation. My apologies, by the way, Dari. I know you put a lot of work into that parchment."

"It doesn't matter," I said. "With the scroll we can start again and do a new translation. Since everyone thinks it's gone, there won't be anyone trying to stop us."

Bartholomew shook his head. "No, Deirdre. That's the one condition I place on you for accepting the scroll. You cannot translate it again. It must be our secret that it survived. Keep it hidden, keep it safe, as Christian women have for centuries."

"But why, Bartholomew?" I asked. "You read it, didn't you? You saw that it poses no threat to the church."

"You know better than that," he replied. "Everything I said to you at Glendalough is still true. That gospel would cause enormous trouble for the church that we can't afford right now. I think Mary herself would agree that the time isn't right for her story to be known. I'm trusting you, Deirdre. I will do everything I can in Rome to protect your monastery and work at Kildare. But if you publish that gospel, all that Brigid and the rest of you have built will come crashing down. I won't be able to stop the forces that will be arrayed against you. So I repeat, however much it goes against your nature, you must keep it secret."

"I hate to admit it, but you're probably right," I said. "But Bartholomew, you do believe these are the words of Mary, don't you?"

"I do," he answered. "That's why I didn't burn the scroll. I couldn't bring myself to destroy a story told by the mother of Jesus herself. You were right, Deirdre. I thought of my wife and daughter when I read it and what they would say if they were still alive to speak to me."

He stood up and brushed the dirt from his robes. We stood with him. He embraced Dari, then me, kissing us both on the cheek.

"I'm leaving you now and heading back to Rome. You should make it safely to Kildare if you move quickly."

He started out across the meadow, but stopped a few feet away. He turned and spoke to us one last time. "Deirdre, I do hope that someday the world can hear the story that Mary tells in that scroll. Someday, when the world is a different place. Until then, keep it safe."

Then he was gone.

"Do you think he'll be all right?" Dari asked.

"Yes, though there will be those at Rome who side with the abbot against him. But I think we now have a friend with the pope's ear."

"As long as we keep the gospel secret."

"Yes."

"Can you do that, Deirdre?"

"I think so. I don't want to bring the wrath of the church down on our monastery. I'll explain everything to Sister Anna and Father Ailbe. I think they'll agree that the time isn't right."

I took Dari's hand in mine. "Are you all right? You almost died this morning because of me."

"So what else is new?" She smiled. It was good to see the light coming back into her eyes. "Life with you is an adventure, Deirdre. I suppose it always will be. But I wouldn't have it any other way."

I squeezed her hand. "We should get moving. The abbot is going to be very angry at us. I have the feeling we haven't seen the last of him."

We put our satchels on our shoulders.

"It's a long walk back to Kildare." She sighed.

"Then we better get going."

I took her arm in mine and we set out together through the meadow toward home.

Author's Note

T he New Testament provides a very incomplete picture of the life of Mary, the mother of Jesus. This became an irresistible invitation for writers through the ages to imagine what the life of this remarkable woman must have been like. There are many stories about Mary in the early Christian tradition, including one that she went to the city of Ephesus on the Aegean coast of modern Turkey to live with the apostle John, to whom Jesus entrusted her as he hung on the cross. But there is another ancient tradition recorded in Egypt and Rome that after the death of her son, Mary lived out the long years of her life with his women followers near Jerusalem.

During the ministry of Jesus and in the first decades of Christianity, women were among the most loyal and influential members of the new faith. They achieved positions of leadership and power, even becoming priests in some branches of the early church. The apostle Paul records in his letters that Christian women throughout the Roman Empire spoke with strong and respected voices in the church. This age of equality between the sexes in Christianity soon faded away with the rise of a dominant male priesthood, but the key role of women in the formative years of the faith cannot be denied.

The Gospel of Mary is a work of fiction, but it is based as closely as possible on biblical, historical, and archaeological sources of what life would have been like for a Jewish peasant woman and her family in Palestine during the tumultuous and violent era of Roman rule. In my description of sixth-century Ireland, I have also tried to be as faithful as possible to what we know about the world in which Sister Deirdre would have lived. The places she visits on her journey across Ireland, including Clare Island, Armagh, and the beautiful valley of Glendalough, are still there for all to visit.

Many thanks to my friends and colleagues for their support in this, the third of the Sister Deirdre novels. Joëlle Delbourgo as always has been the best of literary agents. My gratitude also to Maia Larson and the wonderful team at Pegasus Books for all their help. Thanks as well to the helpful and generous librarians and guides at the National Library of Ireland and the National Museum in Dublin, along with the staff of Wicklow Mountains National Park and the friendly townspeople of Kildare, Ireland, where the remains of the ancient church of Saint Brigid stand even today.